Faux Life

E. A. Rappaport

Owl King Publishing, LLC
Orange, CT

Faux Life

ISBN: 978-1-941042-13-7 (Paperback)

Library of Congress Control Number: 2021946061

First Owl King Publishing Edition: September 2021

Acknowledgments

Cover painting by:
Kamui Ayami

Special thanks to:
Irma Rappaport

Please visit **http://www.owlking.com** for other great fantasy novels and comic books

For My Daughter, Hannah

Contents

Chapter I

A Teenager's Secret

A new morning and a new school awaited, but Victoria wanted to remain asleep. Her pesky alarm clock had other plans. She smacked the snooze button a second time. Unfortunately, a ray of sunshine had already broken through her shades. The world refused to let her dream, but if she stayed in bed, she could avoid the day's problems. No one would care.

"Victoria, come down and eat." Her mom's shout echoed from the kitchen.

Every day, her mother awoke early to prepare breakfast for the family. Although the bacon and eggs smelled delicious, they weren't enough to compensate for Victoria's first day of high school. Not even close. Her stomach disagreed, a sharp pang urging her to listen to her mother. She threw the covers off her body and swiveled her legs off the bed, keeping her head on the pillow as long as possible. Her foot landed in a cardboard box of clothes, which she kicked away before forcing herself into a sitting position.

"It's getting late, honey. You'll be tardy on your first day."

Who cared? Arriving five minutes late wouldn't be terrible. What could be urgent after returning from summer vacation? Introductions? Victoria hated being the center of attention. She'd rather sneak into class another day. No fanfare, no questions.

After stretching her arms, she opened the shades, allowing sunlight to flood the room. All her clothes were jammed into boxes or strewn across the floor. Why bother putting anything away? Victoria hadn't decided if she wanted to live here yet. Although this bedroom was bigger than her old one, it felt foreign. Unpacking her belongings might help, but she'd lived in the other house since she was born. It would take years before she considered this her home. She gazed through the window. A pair of crab apple trees separated her yard from the neighbors, and an old swing set stood in the center of the lawn. The chains holding the wooden swings creaked in the wind.

Victoria moved to the mirror and stared at herself. Her brown eyes begged her to return to bed, but she pursed her lips and picked up a hairbrush, the scar on her arm hidden beneath a thin layer of concealer. Attending a new school might offer her a fresh start. She brushed her hair, which had grown two inches past her shoulder. After a few strokes, a clump of chestnut strands weaved through the hairbrush. She ran her hand through the bristles and dropped the hair onto the floor before completing another twenty strokes.

Her stomach gurgled. Although nervous about school, she was hungry enough for an extra serving this morning.

"Don't forget to make your bed," her mother shouted.

Tossing the brush onto her dresser, Victoria glimpsed the clock. Six-fifty already—she didn't have time to clean her room and eat breakfast. She needed help to complete the chore. Raising her palm upward, she concentrated on the pillows lying against the headboard. Two arms popped out of each pillow, and legs formed at the bottom. The creatures stood motionless, awaiting her command.

"Make the bed," she said and headed downstairs.

Behind her, the pillows marched across the mattress, grabbed the top sheet, and pulled it toward the headboard. Victoria smiled over her shoulder to thank them. They'd remain animated just long enough to finish the task before reverting to normal.

Victoria wasn't sure when she was first able to animate objects. Perhaps the accident had granted her this ability, or she might have been born with it. Either way, she was different from everyone else, but if no one discovered her secret, she could pretend to be a student with standard teenage troubles.

She rushed to the kitchen, where her brother Eli and her father had finished half of their breakfast. Her mom shuffled between the counter and the range, juggling several dishes. When her mom placed her food on the table, Victoria slipped into her seat without making eye contact and dug into the fried eggs.

"I don't have time for a big breakfast," she said. "The bus will be here soon."

"As long as you eat something," said her mom. "Otherwise, you'll be hungry all day. Are you excited about meeting new people?"

"Excited isn't the word I'd use."

"Don't worry, honey. Just be yourself, and you'll make friends."

"Not if she acts weird," Eli said with his face buried in his bowl of cereal.

"You're the weird one, you little monster." Victoria gave his hair a friendly tease.

She never understood why he preferred a bowl of sweet mush to a plate of hot eggs, but if he was happy, he could eat what he wanted.

"Enough bickering." Her father sipped his coffee without lowering the newspaper. "I'm reading."

The article facing Victoria mentioned a drunk driving manslaughter case going to trial in a few months. Victoria kept her head down as she gobbled her food, unable to savor a single tangy bite of bacon.

"Is that the bus?" Her mom held the curtain aside. "Good luck today."

Victoria leaped out of her chair, grabbed her backpack from the hallway floor, and rushed out. A bright yellow bus streaked past her walkway before stopping at the corner. Victoria ran toward the vehicle, waving her arms and shouting. Another second and she would have been late for school. Her backpack knocked into the "For Sale" sign on the lawn, causing the smaller "Sold" sign to fall halfway off its hinges. Both signs had to come down. Why advertise that they'd just moved, inviting everyone over to meet the neighbors?

Victoria increased her pace. Thankfully, the bus door remained open until she reached the stop. She stepped inside with a broad smile, returned only by the driver, an older man sporting grizzled hair and aviator glasses. The students had paired up in the seats, staring at their phones. She wasn't surprised. It was no different in her former hometown. A movie star could have strutted on board and not received a single glance. As the bus rolled forward, Victoria traipsed down the aisle and deposited herself in the back seat. With everyone distracted, she wasn't going to meet anyone until they arrived at school. She shrugged, took out her own phone, and joined the crowd.

The short ride ended in front of Shelley High School. Several glass and concrete wings reached out from the primary structure, extending halfway to the athletic fields, while three parking lots encroached on a nearby forest. This campus was easily twice the size of her elementary and middle schools combined.

Dozens of students dawdled on the lawn with their friends, enjoying their freedom before the day began. Apparently, cliques had already formed, probably carried over from last year. Clusters of similarly dressed boys and girls had gravitated toward one another. Victoria wondered if they'd discussed their outfits beforehand, or if their clothes dictated their personality. Last year, she hadn't noticed special groups. She hung out with friends and didn't care how others viewed her. In high school, however, she wouldn't survive on her own. To fit in, she'd have to dress like everyone else.

"This year won't be too bad," said the bus driver. "You're not alone."

His voice startled Victoria. No one else was on the bus. A warm flush traveled through her cheeks as she slung her backpack over her shoulder. Why delay the inevitable? This was her opportunity to redefine herself. Nobody would recognize her, so she could join any group. After forcing a smile onto her face, she hopped off the bus.

Her first few steps carried her toward some athletic girls, probably expecting to join the volleyball team. Although tall and thin, Victoria had never excelled at sports. She veered away, eyeing a few students wearing fancy blouses and skirts. The girls laughed while they talked, displaying the sheer joy of being together. Before Victoria reached them, the first bell rang.

Slowly, the kids filtered through the school doors, filling the bright hallway with a crowd so thick Victoria couldn't see the room numbers. The students moved in small packs, none of them glancing at her. On the rare occasion when she smiled at a friendly face, the others refused to acknowledge her existence. She didn't need everyone to notice her, but a simple greeting would have been welcome. Perhaps it would be easier to introduce herself after the excitement of seeing old friends had died down. Why rush to join a clique before first period?

Victoria fished through her backpack for her school map but couldn't find it in the jumble of papers. She'd brought school transfer documents, notes about her summer reading, and more blank paper than was necessary. When she looked up, the students had disappeared into their respective rooms.

An attractive girl with raven hair smiled from down the hall. Victoria returned the cheerful greeting, wondering how to introduce herself. Her heart fluttered. Perhaps she would make a new friend before school started. This year might not be so bad.

The other girl strolled toward Victoria, still grinning.

"Hi, I'm..."

Victoria stopped talking as the other girl shuffled past without a peek. Her stomach sank. The smile hadn't been for her. A blonde girl who'd been standing behind Victoria the whole time wrapped her arms around her friend.

"Where were you all summer?" asked the dark-haired girl.

"With the family in Europe." The blonde girl rolled her eyes. "You know how they can be. I'm glad to be back."

"Yeah, families are such a bore."

The two girls entered the nearest classroom, leaning on each other for support. Couldn't they walk on their own? Victoria had known girls like those. Heard their laughter, their ridicule. Would it have been so difficult for them to give her a nod? They deserved a reminder that they weren't so special. The dark-haired girl's pocketbook was open, displaying her compact and a tube of bright red lipstick. Victoria raised her palm and concentrated on the two items until each of them grew a pair of feet.

"Go have fun," she whispered.

The tiny creatures jumped out of the pocketbook and ran through the hallway, leaving a trail of red and beige behind. Victoria immediately regretted her action. Maybe the girls didn't greet her because they hadn't seen each other for weeks. Victoria might have acted similarly if the situation were reversed. She promised herself to be more patient in the future.

Her geometry classroom wasn't far. When the second bell rang, the teacher hadn't arrived, but the whiteboard held the message "Welcome, Freshmen." Students had filled half the seats, giving Victoria several possibilities, but she had to choose wisely. Where she sat today might define her for the rest of high school. A front seat would make her appear too studious, but sitting in back meant she wasn't interested in learning. Victoria selected a spot behind two attractive girls. She slid into the chair, shoved her backpack under the desk, and listened to their conversation.

"Where'd you get that top?" asked the girl in front, her perfect hair held together with copious amounts of spray.

Victoria leaned forward but couldn't detect any chemical odor, only sweet blossoms. These girls might make good friends if she proved she belonged in their group.

"Where do you think?" The other girl's braids bounced as she spoke.

"Must have been expensive."

"I guess. Let's go shopping after school. My clothes are so last year."

Victoria looked down at her shirt, wincing at a dark stain near the hem. A moving box must have rubbed against her. She tucked the stain into her pants, hoping nobody noticed. Those girls weren't the only ones who needed to go shopping.

"Good morning, students," said the teacher, a young woman with short brown hair and a pair of thick glasses. "We're going to have an exciting year."

Victoria didn't need exciting. She needed uneventful.

Chapter II

Shopping for a good Fit

Instead of going home after school, Victoria walked to the nearest transit bus stop, a couple of blocks away. Public transportation here was better than in the rural town where she grew up. Electric buses looped around the principal thoroughfares, allowing easy travel to any part of town. Victoria couldn't believe so few people took advantage of this service.

A hefty woman boarded the bus at the next stop and sat beside Victoria, taking up most of the seat. Victoria squeezed closer to the window and stared at the road. Strip malls and diners replaced acres of farmland, while street lamps and sidewalks lined the roadways. Traveling by car was more comfortable, but riding the bus was much safer. When they passed a supermarket, Victoria remembered that her mother had asked her to buy bread and milk on the way home. She wrote a note to herself and shoved it into her backpack. With all her daily responsibilities, she didn't understand how adults had time to do anything they enjoyed.

Several stops later, the bus arrived at a mall larger than Victoria's old town center. Four department stores framed a three-story monstrosity, housing two hundred shops and a dozen restaurants. The size of the place overwhelmed Victoria, almost convincing her to return to a small strip mall along the route. Perhaps a cheap knockoff blouse would be sufficient. Her eyes ventured to the stain on her shirt, reminding her of this important mission. The fashionable girls would spot the difference in quality. She took a deep breath and marched into the building.

Even on a weekday afternoon, frenzied shoppers filled the mall. Victoria imagined that many of them lived here, eating at the food court and sleeping on empty benches. It wouldn't have been the worst existence. They were never alone, maintenance workers cleaned the bathrooms every day, and the temperature never varied.

A quick sweep of the lower level led her past dozens of shops offering toys, electronics, and sports equipment. Victoria ignored them and rode the escalator to the second floor. Along the way, she watched people scramble between the stores, searching for new possessions. Was impressing the popular girls so important that she had to join the mall crowd? The escalator deposited her in front of a department store's perfume section, where a noxious cloud of sweet, flowery, and musky scents wafted over her. Holding her nose, she scurried away.

After passing a shop dedicated to expensive shoes, Victoria approached a trendy boutique. Most people gaped at the overpriced merchandise through the windows instead of entering. With a nervous smile, Victoria strolled inside and headed to a rack of gorgeous tops. To balance her budget, she'd have to forgo other spending for a while, but this purchase was necessary. A young woman approached her before she touched the nearest blouse.

"May I help you?" the clerk asked, eyeing her closely.

"Where are the changing rooms?"

"In the back." The clerk pointed past some mirrors. "Please leave your backpack with me."

No wonder she was pretending to be helpful. She assumed a girl with stained clothing and a heavy backpack would be a shoplifter. Normally, the insult would have convinced Victoria to patronize a different store, but she had to buy an outfit like the other girls wore. This meant swallowing her pride and ignoring the suspicious clerk.

"Thank you." She handed over her backpack. "I'll let you know if I need anything else."

The clerk held the backpack away from her body as if it was infested with lice, before depositing it behind the counter. Victoria was ready to give up on this store, but she recognized a flowery blouse. If the popular girls shopped here, then so would she.

The rack displayed dozens of gorgeous tops. Victoria selected a few and carefully draped them over her arm for the brief trip to the dressing room. She shouldn't have considered anything this expensive. A single blouse was more than she'd spent on her entire wardrobe, but it was worth an easy-in with the popular girls. She moved to another rack and selected an armful of skirts to match the tops.

At the back of the store, a middle-aged woman exited the changing rooms carrying a mound of dresses, probably gifts for her daughter to start the school year. Why hadn't the woman brought her daughter? Victoria enjoyed her late August shopping sprees with her mom. Perhaps they should have come together today, but she was too eager to pick up her new outfits.

On her way to the changing room, Victoria gave the woman a polite nod, excited to try on the clothes. When they within three feet of each other, the woman tripped on a dress she was carrying and collided with Victoria. Clothing flew everywhere as she knocked Victoria into a rack.

"I'm so sorry." The woman stretched her hand toward Victoria. "Let me help you up."

"Don't you look where you're going?" Victoria avoided contact with the clumsy woman. "Someone could get hurt."

She snatched her blouses from the floor before the woman touched them and continued toward the dressing room.

"I told you I was sorry." The woman helped the clerk return the rack to its original position. "It was an accident."

Victoria didn't turn back, furious at the woman's lack of coordination. What if a skirt had ripped? The mean clerk would have blamed Victoria and forced her to pay for the damaged item. Thankfully, the accident had only wrinkled the outfits.

Inside the dressing room, Victoria tried on each combination of top and skirt, selecting the three best pairs to purchase. It wasn't enough to replace her wardrobe, but it was a start.

She peeked out from the dressing room to confirm the middle-aged woman was gone. Victoria regretted being curt with her and didn't want to cross paths again. She also hoped the mean clerk's shift was over, but the girl was tending the checkout counter. After a deep breath to calm herself, Victoria approached the register, placed the clothing down, and handed her a credit card.

"This your mom's card, hon?" asked the clerk. "You can't use it without her."

"It's mine." Victoria reached over the counter for her backpack.

The clerk stepped back, not helping her lug the heavy pack over the counter. Victoria dug through the front pocket until she found her school ID card and held it in front of the clerk's face. After a mumble of disapproval, the young lady rang up the items and handed Victoria the receipt. It would take months of odd jobs to pay down the card.

Victoria left the mall with a bag of clothing and a vow never to return unless her friends forced her to go. She hopped onto the bus, sporting a satisfied grin. Her first day had been productive.

The next morning, Victoria sprang from bed, eager to meet new friends. She'd never been interested in fashion, but her expensive outfit gave her the confidence to approach the popular group. Maybe after school, she'd join them flipping through style magazines for tips. Homework would have to wait.

After a quick breakfast, Victoria reached the bus stop with minutes to spare. Throughout the ride, she kept fidgeting as she wondered how to introduce herself. Clare and Belle knew her name from roll call in class, but she had to impress them the first time they spoke. They must have known she'd recently moved into town, so her newcomer status would give her an excuse for wearing a grungy outfit yesterday. It took time to unpack after moving to a different house. Excitement turned to nervousness as the bus drew closer to the school. If it weren't for her new clothing, she might have given up on her plan.

Clare and Belle stood within a circle of girls, each one wearing an outfit that could have graced the cover of a teen magazine. Victoria threw her shoulders back and marched toward the group, telling herself that she belonged with them. At first, the outer circle of girls didn't budge, but when they shifted positions to let in someone else, Victoria squeezed through their ranks.

Talking stopped as both Clare and Belle gazed at her. This was her chance for a spectacular year at school. Victoria opened her mouth to introduce herself when Belle reached around her back and touched her shirt. Victoria craned her head to the side and glimpsed the edge of a price tag between Belle's fingers. Her heart skipped a beat.

"If you want to buy your way into our group," said Belle, "take the tags off first. What were you going to do? Return the blouse after we accepted you?"

The group laughed as they flowed around Victoria on their way toward the school entrance. A wave of embarrassment rose through her body, ending with a rush of anger. Victoria grabbed the price tag and tore it off the shirt. She didn't care if she ripped a hole in the expensive blouse. It was worthless.

As the other girls neared the front door, Victoria eyed an open garbage can containing a banana peel nearby. She could redirect their mocking from her to someone else. As she stepped closer to the trash, she held out her hand and focused on the mottled peel. The banana creature could trip one of the girls or cling to her leg until she was in front of a class. Either way, the laughter toward Victoria would end.

"Forget them," came a voice from behind. "They're not worth the trouble."

Victoria lost her concentration on the banana before it could animate. A girl with long black hair approached her.

"I'm Hannah." The new girl snipped the plastic tag holder off Victoria's shirt with a nail clipper. "I watched you move in the other day."

Although she was shorter than Victoria, her thin limbs made her appear tall. A plaid skirt flowed out from below a green cardigan, while a pair of tan booties completed the look. In stark contrast to the popular girls' fashionable outfits, Hannah's clothes appeared to have been around for a decade.

"You were spying on me?" asked Victoria.

"No, I didn't mean…" A furrowed brow replaced Hannah's smile. "I saw the moving truck…"

"I was kidding." Victoria grinned. "Thanks for calming me down. Those girls made me so angry."

Hannah led her toward the school.

"I was about to introduce myself after school yesterday," she said, "but you disappeared before getting on the bus."

Victoria stared at her blouse, ready to tear it off her body. If it weren't against the dress code, she would have tossed it in the trash with the banana.

"I went shopping." She stepped through the doorway. "Now I have to return what I bought. No point in keeping this anymore."

"But the blouse looks cute on you," said Hannah. "With or without the tag."

Although Victoria's trip to the mall didn't get her into the popular group, it resulted in gaining a new friend. Perhaps her expensive clothing wasn't so bad after all.

When the first bell rang, Victoria and Hannah hurried toward their first classes, separating halfway down the hall.

"Lunch?" Hannah asked from her classroom doorway.

Victoria answered with a smile.

All cafeterias looked familiar. A line of kids stretched out the door, with students waiting to drop unappetizing grub onto their trays. Cliques had reserved half of the tables, while one teacher attempted to control the ever-increasing noise. Victoria stood behind some upperclassmen, more interested in chatting about their summer vacation than eating lunch. Eventually she reached the front of the line and chose a slice of soggy pizza with a side order of pale fries. A few more days of this dreck and she might bring her own food.

She roamed the cafeteria until she found Hannah at a table populated with a few quiet boys. Victoria sat across from her new friend, who'd already finished most of a peanut butter and jelly sandwich. A handful of carrot sticks and a mound of potato chips sat atop Hannah's flattened brown paper bag, with a thermos nearby.

"I don't blame you for bringing lunch," said Victoria. "This stuff doesn't look good."

"I bet it tastes just as bad." Hannah munched on a carrot. "I prefer to know what I'm eating, regardless if it's disgusting or delicious."

"What's not to know?" Victoria held up the sagging pizza slice and bit into the end. "It's exactly what it looks like, although it should be hotter. It didn't burn my mouth."

Hannah reached for a french fry, pausing for confirmation.

"You sure it's not too much of a mystery?" asked Victoria.

"What can you do to a potato?"

"Go for it," said Victoria, "in exchange for carrot sticks. Wanna try the pizza?"

"No thanks. I like mine with onions and olives."

"Pepperoni's my favorite," said Victoria.

"Never tried it." Hannah took a bite of her sandwich. "I've been vegetarian since I can remember."

Victoria crunched down on the carrots, catching a boy staring at her when she looked up. He quickly returned his gaze to his friends.

"Don't worry about Brandon and the others," Hannah whispered. "They'll leave us alone. They never talked to girls in middle school."

"You seem to know about everyone. Did you spy on them, too?"

Hannah choked on her last bite before washing it down with a gulp of water.

"I wasn't spying on you," she said. "I live across the street, three houses down. It was the first moving van in the neighborhood."

"Nothing ever changed where I used to live," Victoria said with a wistful smile. "I've only seen moving trucks on the highway. My nearest neighbors must have owned their house since the turn of the last century."

"Well, I'm glad you moved here instead of centenarians." Hannah finished the rest of her food. "So we can hang out together. How about after school to study?"

"I'm still unpacking," said Victoria. "Another day."

"Do you mean that?" asked Hannah. "Or are you being polite?"

"No, I meant it." Victoria offered her more fries. She couldn't lose her new friend so soon. "Give me time to get settled."

"I can help you unpack." Hannah passed on the food. "I'm an excellent organizer."

"My mom would never allow guests if the house wasn't spotless," said Victoria. "You know how crazy parents can be."

"Sure, my mom won't let me take driving lessons until I'm eighteen. It's going to be embarrassing when everyone else drives to school, and I'm the only one on the bus."

"I'll take the bus with you," said Victoria. "I promise."

"To bus buddies." Hannah tapped Victoria's milk carton with her thermos and took a sip.

Victoria sighed in relief before scarfing down the rest of her lunch, happy she found a new friend.

After lunch, they headed for class together. English was a difficult subject for Victoria, so she was glad they were in the same class. The teacher, an outspoken young woman, had encouraged participation in group discussions, giving it a separate grade during each marking period. Victoria expected to fail that portion of the class, but with Hannah next to her, she might receive a passing mark.

While waiting for the teacher, the volume of chatter increased by the second. She might have forgotten about the class. Most of the kids would have welcomed a free period, but Hannah sat back in her chair with a faint grin.

"Why are you smiling?" asked Victoria.

"Everyone will be so upset when she brings the books."

"What books?"

"*A Tale of Two Cities*."

Victoria had checked the curriculum online, and there'd been no mention of a reading list. She assumed the teacher hadn't finalized the course, but Hannah must have known something different.

"How do you know what's first?" asked Victoria. "Did she post the coursework today?"

"I haven't checked the curriculum since last weekend," said Hannah, "but she was walking toward the library when we left the cafeteria."

"She could have been going anywhere. Even if it was the library, she could have selected any books."

"I have study hall in the library." Hannah placed a thin notebook in front of her next to a mechanical pencil. "The books were piled behind the librarian."

"Those could have been for any class."

"Doubtful," said Hannah. "The cafeteria lady asked our teacher if it was the best of times. She said she'd find out soon enough. Didn't you hear them talking on the way out?"

"I was trying to keep that disgusting food down," said Victoria. "Maybe tomorrow they'll offer something palatable."

"Here she comes," Hannah said moments before the teacher entered the room carrying a stack of paperbacks.

She was right about the books. Perhaps this friendship was too dangerous. With Hannah so observant, Victoria would have to be careful not to use her special ability anywhere within sight.

Chapter III

A Near Miss

The first couple of school weeks flew by, especially because Victoria had four classes with Hannah. Between cultivating her friendship, completing her homework, and becoming familiar with the neighborhood, she didn't meet anyone else in school. Victoria didn't mind, however, because she'd grown close to Hannah. There was an important difference between fitting in with a crowd and having a genuine friend.

After lunch, Victoria walked to English class with Hannah, talking about the confusing first chapters of *A Tale of Two Cities*. They arrived in the classroom to find a note on the board assigning extra homework. Victoria groaned at the sight. After finally settling into a decent routine, she had more work to finish. Fitting another two hours of studying into her schedule was impossible.

"Don't worry," said Hannah. "She's assigning the work because tomorrow's a day off."

"What? I didn't know about that. Is it some professional development thing for the teachers?"

"Tomorrow is 'Bring your child to work' day."

"But the calendar didn't show school was closed." Victoria fished through her overflowing backpack but couldn't find her day planner. "I'm sure of it."

"School's not officially closed," said Hannah. "Some students go to work with their parents, but the rest don't come to class. Why not enjoy a free day when the weather's decent?"

Victoria shoved the papers back down. The front flap didn't reach far enough for the clasps to lock.

"'Bring your child to work day' was in the spring at my old school," she said.

"Yeah, things are different around here." Hannah took her seat next to Victoria. "This school doesn't have a valedictorian, only a group of academic achievers. Like we don't know who gets the best grades in class."

"So we don't have to try as hard, but someone will always be the best, no matter what they call it."

A pile of papers popped out of Victoria's backpack when she took out her notebook. She squeezed everything back in and left the clasps open.

"You going to work with your parents tomorrow?" asked Hannah.

"Nah, my dad makes sales calls from home nowadays, and my mom takes care of the house. How about you?"

"My mom's an accountant," said Hannah. "Sitting around an office looking at numbers doesn't interest me. Can we hang out tomorrow?"

"I'll just come to school." Victoria opened her notebook to the English section and placed her pencil on her desk. "If I have extra homework, I might as well finish it here. It'll be quieter than at my house."

"Then I'll come to school with you," said Hannah. "The weather's supposed to be nice. Let's walk instead of taking the bus. We might get there a few minutes late, but no one will care."

"Or we could leave earlier and arrive on time."

"I suppose so." Hannah had a separate notebook for each subject, all fitting neatly into her backpack. "Ten minutes early would push it for me. I'm not as much of a morning person as you are."

Victoria wouldn't have called herself a morning person. Her suggestion was to get them to class on time, not because she enjoyed less sleep. Hannah didn't know her too well.

"Deal," she said. "I'll wait for you on the corner."

The next morning, Victoria's beeping alarm clock didn't bother her as much as usual. She only swiped the snooze button once before getting out of bed, scarfing down a big breakfast, and trotting to the corner. A chorus of birds chirped in the bushes, and five squirrels scurried around the yards, occasionally venturing into the street toward better scavenging locations. The sun had risen an hour ago, dissipating the morning chill, but a pack of gray clouds loomed over the horizon, threatening rain later.

At the end of each driveway, garbage cans released a mixture of odors, from rotting food to sweaty socks. Victoria found a spot upwind from the worst offenders. Several minutes later, Hannah slogged up the street with her eyes on her feet. She eked out a smile when she locked eyes with Victoria.

"You look tired," said Victoria.

"I could sleep another two hours," said Hannah. "But that's not the worst part of my morning. My mom was hoping I'd go to work with her. She said I could do homework in the office if staring at numbers bored me."

"Maybe she didn't want you hanging out with me."

"She hasn't met you yet." Hannah took the lead on the sidewalk. "And when she does, she's sure to like you. She just wanted company for a day. I bet she's bored at work. Math is bad enough for one period. I can't imagine it as a career."

Victoria jogged at her side.

"You should go with her." She scooted in front and stopped. "Don't let her down today. Anything can happen in the future."

"What is that supposed to mean?"

"She... in a few years we'll be off at college." Victoria peeked back at her house. "Your mom might want to spend time with you while she can."

She would have loved if her father had brought her to work, but he always thought school was more important. He told her that she'd spend a lifetime in an office but only a few years in school.

"My mom will be fine." Hannah nudged Victoria forward. "If she wanted to do something fun with me, she'd take the day off. Even if I went with her, she'd spend hours on the computer. Besides, you and I made our plans first."

"I guess." Victoria added a spring to her step, glad that Hannah had chosen her.

Several blocks up the street, a group of younger kids stared at their cellphones, fingers furiously pressing against the screens to garner the highest score on whatever game was most popular this week. Victoria hadn't owned a phone until a couple of years ago, yet the kids up ahead were clearly in elementary school. They didn't realize how privileged they were.

Behind her, an engine revved from down the road. It had to be a car racing to make a red light. Victoria peeked over her shoulder. A gray sedan sped toward her, while the driver texted on his phone. As he zoomed past, Victoria shouted at him to pay attention, but his eyes remained down as his car swerved back and forth.

The noise must have distracted one of the young boys. He tripped on the curb and fell into the street. Victoria raised her palm upward, stared at the nearest garbage cans, and concentrated. Feet grew from the bottoms of the cans and launched them into the street, causing a loud clang. Garbage spread out from the bins. The kids jumped backward toward the nearest lawn, and the car veered to the other side.

"Yeah, you better watch where you're going," Victoria shouted.

"What just happened?" Hannah grabbed Victoria's shoulders. "You saved those kids somehow. I was looking at those cans. Nothing pushed them."

"You're talking nonsense." Victoria shrugged her off. "That crazy driver nearly ruined the lives of several families. Luckily, a squirrel knocked a garbage can in front of him. Nothing but sheer luck. Unfortunately, he won't learn from his mistake because no one was injured."

"I didn't see any stray squirrels." Hannah rushed forward. "The cans fell over themselves. I'm sure of it."

"Maybe a kid bumped into them by accident.

Victoria dashed ahead of Hannah, grabbed the cans, and forced them back into their natural state before returning them to the curb.

"See? Nothing strange about these."

Victoria shuffled down the road, increasing her pace as she went.

"But I saw you do the same motion with your hand when we met." Hannah rushed to keep up. "You were going to punish those girls for laughing at you."

"You must be thinking about something else."

"I'll never tell anyone," said Hannah. "In case you change your mind and want to discuss it."

"There's nothing to talk about." Victoria kept going without looking back. "Hurry, or we'll be late for the bell."

She'd misjudged how long it would take to walk to school. The delay with the garbage cans was only a couple of minutes, yet the buses were leaving when they arrived on campus. The first bell had already rung, giving them seconds before class started. No other students were in sight as they hurried through the open doors. In the front office, the clock read half past seven. The second bell would ring at any moment.

"Turn it back two minutes," said Hannah. "Or we'll get in trouble for being tardy."

"What? I can't change the clock from here."

Hannah's sudden stop caused Victoria to bump into her.

"Please," said Hannah. "Do it for me."

"It's the beginning of the school year," said Victoria. "Even if we're late for class, nothing will happen. Besides, you told me it didn't matter if we arrived late."

As soon as the bell rang, a tall man in a steel gray suit stepped out of the office. His neatly trimmed hair made his head appear square, and his neck disappeared in his shirt. Victoria saw a reflection of herself in his spotless shoes.

"Mr. Moritz, the vice principal," said Hannah, "formerly the principal of the middle school. I wasn't the most... punctual student last year."

He marched closer and handed a folded note to Hannah. She knew what it said, because she didn't bother looking at it. Victoria, however, glimpsed impeccable handwriting, fancy enough for a wedding invitation. It was a detention slip for Friday.

"But we were late because we saved a kid's life," said Hannah. "A car would have hit him if we didn't do something."

"I don't care if you saved the president's life," said Mr. Moritz. "You must be in class at seven-thirty sharp. Arrive on time or suffer the consequences."

He turned his harsh stare to Victoria, sending a chill through her body.

"This is your only warning, young lady," he said. "No exceptions."

Victoria's heart sank into her stomach. She'd never gotten into trouble before, yet she'd received a warning within the first month of school. It felt like she wasn't in control of her actions. She wanted to promise this wouldn't happen again, but no words came out of her mouth.

"Why are you still standing here?" Mr. Moritz glared at her. "Get to class already."

Victoria rushed to her first period, without a glance at Hannah.

After school on Friday, Victoria sat in the library finishing her geometry homework. She remained seated and quiet for an hour while the rest of the students prepared for the weekend. It wouldn't have mattered if Mr. Moritz had given her a detention. Weekends were nothing special, and ever since meeting Hannah, she preferred to be in school together.

With a few minutes to go before the detention period ended, Victoria jammed her geometry papers into her backpack. The canvas was stretched so tightly that it seemed one more paper would cause it to burst open. Other kids didn't lug around so much with them, but what if they needed something they'd discarded? Victoria slung the pack over her shoulder, adjusting the weight on her back before trudging to the detention room.

Hannah was sitting at a desk three rows ahead of the other kids, all with their heads buried in papers.

"Detention is over." The teacher closed the book she was reading and pushed away from the desk. "Try to stay out of trouble this weekend."

Most of the kids darted away, nearly knocking Victoria over in their rush to escape. Hannah placed her homework in her backpack and joined Victoria near the desk.

"You didn't have to stay in school," she said. "I'm the one who got detention."

"I had to finish the geometry problems, anyway," said Victoria. "Wanna walk home together?"

She shifted her backpack to her other shoulder, causing a few papers to fall out.

"You should clean that out." Hannah bent down to pick up the papers. "How can you find anything in there?"

"I can't." Victoria shoved everything back in and led Hannah toward the front entrance. "Maybe I'll sort through it this weekend."

Hannah followed her out the door, collecting more papers that had fallen from Victoria's backpack. She handed them over, but Victoria didn't replace them, instead just carried them down the street.

"Speaking of this weekend," said Hannah, "it should be fun, don't you think?"

"Why? What's happening?"

"Tomorrow's the annual block party." Hannah picked up another paper and held it out. "The families on our street gather for a day of food, games, and gossip. I can't wait to meet your parents."

"Now that you mention it, I saw a note about the party, but we won't be attending," said Victoria. "We have other plans."

"No, don't make me go another year without a friend at the party," said Hannah. "I can't stand the whispering about who had plastic surgery or whose credit card was denied at the supermarket. Please come. You don't have to stay long."

Victoria preferred not to spend extra time around people who might start rumors, but she couldn't disappoint her friend.

"I'll ask to change our plans," she said.

"Thanks. You'll see—we'll have a great time. We can start our own rumors and see how far they spread."

Victoria gave her a tentative smile. As long as the stories weren't about herself, everything would be fine.

Chapter IV

The Trouble with Neighbors

Victoria had hoped for rain, but no clouds graced the bright blue sky. If she'd possessed the ability to cause a storm, she would have flooded the streets enough to paddle a boat. Instead, she baked a batch of brownies from a box and rummaged through her closet for a decent outfit, having returned the clothes she'd just purchased. They were too expensive anyway. She settled on an old dress that her mother used to wear, its colors faded yet vibrant enough to stand out among the usual tans, browns, and blacks so popular in early fall.

A few houses away, several tables had been set up on the grass between two yards. Young children scampered around the lawn, while older kids and adults played croquet across the street. Victoria didn't recognize anyone except a gray-haired woman who stood behind the dessert table. Mrs. Bailey lived next door and was the only neighbor who'd welcomed her to the new house. Others must have been too busy with their own lives to bother introducing themselves.

Hannah had wanted to meet at noon, but Victoria didn't see her anywhere, although it was still a few minutes early. Judging by the vice principal's treatment of them last week, her friend wasn't the most punctual person. Victoria circled the party, carrying her tray of brownies as a shield against anyone approaching her.

"Are those for my table?" Mrs. Bailey called out when she wandered too close. "You don't have to lug them around all day. Put them here with the desserts and go mingle."

Victoria smiled at her as she deposited the aluminum tray between a mound of chocolate chip cookies and a pair of apple pies. The sweet aroma made Victoria's mouth water. She might have to skip lunch and sample each of the desserts instead.

"Those brownies look delicious," said Mrs. Bailey. "Did you bake them yourself?"

"Yes, but not from scratch," said Victoria. "I used a mix."

"Shh." Mrs. Bailey put her finger in front of her mouth. "No one needs to know they're not real. It'll be our little secret."

She peered over Victoria's shoulder.

"Are your parents coming?" she asked. "I've been meaning to introduce myself, but sometimes I get wrapped up in my own life. You know how it is between school and friends and family. There's never enough time to do everything we want."

"It's just me today," said Victoria. "They were hoping to come, but they're under the weather."

"I'm sorry to hear that." Mrs. Bailey cut a large slice from a pie. "It's too early for cold and flu season, but some pie should help them feel better."

"Thanks," said Victoria. "It can't hurt."

"I'm glad you didn't catch their cold," said Mrs. Bailey. "Tell your mom to stop by when she's better. We have much to talk about."

"I promise." Victoria took the plate just as a younger couple arrived at the table.

Mrs. Bailey chatted with them about their son and his new kindergarten friends. She seemed knowledgeable about the local elementary school, but she and her husband owned a small shop downtown. Her information must have come from neighborhood gossip, making her a source of many rumors. Victoria had to be extra careful around her, including keeping the shades closed on her side of the house. She didn't need a nosy neighbor learning about her special ability.

"Don't tell me you ate lunch already." Hannah joined Victoria at the dessert table. "I'm only three minutes late."

"I was just leaving my brownies here." Victoria adjusted her tray's position. "And speaking with Mrs. Bailey."

Hannah greeted Mrs. Bailey while grabbing the largest brownie. She took one bite and said, "From a box?"

"Is it that obvious?"

Hannah nodded and took her by the hand, leading her to the main course table.

"Here, try this." She handed a plate of lasagna to Victoria.

"Did you make this?" asked Victoria. "It smells amazing."

"It's my mom's special lasagna." Hannah grabbed a plate for herself after finishing the brownie and licking the chocolate off her fingers. "You'll love it."

Victoria let her first bite linger in her mouth, savoring the tangy tomato and sharp cheese.

"It tastes even better than it smells." She quickly finished a few more forkfuls. "Your mom could be a chef if she tires of accounting."

"I doubt it," said Hannah. "Everything else she cooks is barely edible. That's why we call this 'special.'"

Victoria chuckled at the joke. She couldn't imagine Hannah's mother not being a wonderful cook if this dish was so delicious. Perhaps Hannah was a picky eater.

"I'm glad your family changed plans this weekend." Hannah gazed around the two yards. "Where are your parents?"

"Our plans changed because they got sick." Victoria dug in for seconds. "Just a common cold, but they didn't want to infect anyone else."

Hannah snatched the tray of lasagna.

"That was thoughtful, but we should bring them food," she said. "It'll make them feel better."

Victoria latched onto the other end of the tray and pulled.

"They're contagious." She tugged again, but Hannah wouldn't let go. "I'll be the next one to catch the cold, but you shouldn't risk getting sick."

"I'm not afraid of a sore throat and sniffles," said Hannah.

"But they'll feel guilty for infecting you," said Victoria. "Here, I'll bring it to them and be right back."

"Fine." Hannah released the food as a frown took over her face. "I'll have more dessert while I wait."

Why did Victoria have to darken her friend's mood? They were getting along so well. She brought the lasagna and pie home and returned quickly. Hannah hadn't moved from the main course table, although more neighbors had surrounded her.

"I haven't met your parents yet." Victoria approached her friend with a hopeful look. "Are they here?"

A bright smile returned to Hannah's face when she pointed to an attractive woman speaking with Mrs. Bailey.

"C'mon, I'll introduce you to my mom."

She pulled Victoria across the yard. Her mother had the same long hair but wore dark pants and a shirt.

"This is my new friend, Victoria," said Hannah. "She just moved in down the street from us."

Victoria held out her hand. "It's nice to meet you, Mrs. Walton. Your special lasagna was the best I ever tasted."

"Thank you. The recipe has been in my family for generations." Hannah's mother stepped backward. "Mrs. Bailey tells me your family is sick. You don't mind if I don't shake your hand. I'm finishing an important project next week, and I can't miss a single day."

She held her arms away with her body tilted backward.

"I understand," Victoria said, glad that Hannah wasn't as germaphobic as her mother.

"After you've all recovered," said Mrs. Walton, "you should come over for dinner."

"Only if you make lasagna." Hannah took Victoria's hand. "They just finished a game of croquet. If we hurry, we can play the next round."

"It was nice to meet you," Victoria called out as she followed Hannah across the street.

Hannah's mother waved back before returning to her conversation with Mrs. Bailey. Victoria watched them, wondering if they were discussing what type of cold was going around the neighborhood. Did it matter? People came down with colds all the time.

Hoops and mallets were scattered across the playing field. The previous participants didn't clean up after they finished. Victoria rolled a few balls toward the center.

"Two people aren't enough players for a game," she said.

"I'm sure a few others will join us." Hannah put her hand on Victoria's shoulder. "You know how to play, right?"

"Yeah, mostly."

"Oh." Hannah's face fell. "Don't you like the game?"

"I'm not too good." Victoria grabbed a mallet and forced a smile. "Let's get ready."

They were soon joined by Mr. and Mrs. Hall, a middle-aged couple living a few doors down; their son Theodore, who was home from college for the weekend; and Mr. Kennedy, an older man from the end of the road.

Mr. Hall squared off against Mr. Kennedy.

"Us against you?" He selected three mallets.

Theodore chose his own color. "How about changing things up this year?"

"Yeah," said Hannah. "Make it a fair game."

After a nod from the rest of the players, they drew sticks to determine the starting order. Victoria was first, giving her a clear disadvantage.

"Aren't you supposed to play in order of the colors on the stake?" she asked, but no one seemed to listen.

"Don't worry about it," said Hannah. "It's your turn."

Victoria knocked her ball through the first two wickets, gaining two extra strokes, but couldn't pass through the third hoop, leaving her ball vulnerable near the side of the playing field. She'd always played croquet in teams, but everyone here wanted to be on their own, including Hannah.

Mr. Hall played next, hitting his ball through the first four wickets with ease. At this rate, it would be a quick game. Mr. Kennedy, however, wasn't about to let anyone else gain too much ground. Instead of trying for the third hoop, he hit Mr. Hall's ball and used his croquet stroke to send it into the next yard. Victoria guessed they were long-time rivals, Mr. Hall's skill evenly matched against Mr. Kennedy's strategy. She wouldn't have been surprised if they'd kept a running score throughout the years.

Hannah was up next, hitting Victoria's ball on her third shot. Victoria expected to be knocked into the neighbor's yard with Mr. Hall, but Hannah hit her ball two feet away, toward the hoop.

"We should help each other, or we'll have no chance to win," she said, "but I have a better idea. Let's start a rumor about Theodore. It might distract Mr. Hall enough to throw him off his game."

"Wouldn't that make it easier for Mr. Kennedy to win?" asked Victoria.

"Not if we teamed up against him." Hannah's last shot put her in line with the third hoop. "We can tell him a car knocked Theodore off his bike at school. He'll eventually bring it up with Mr. Hall."

"I'd never do that." Victoria squeezed her mallet. "How could you make up such a terrible lie? You'll scare his parents."

"Theodore's playing croquet with us. No one would ever think the accident was serious. It would only make Mr. Hall wonder what else his son is hiding. You know, throw him off his game."

"I don't care about winning." Victoria frowned. "Let's just play."

"I was only trying to make it more interesting." Hannah slinked off the playing field. "Last place here we come."

Theodore took his turn, leaving his ball in the middle of the field, and Mrs. Hall was the last up, displaying as much skill as her husband. She hit Theodore's ball, knocked it to the end of the court, and sent her ball through the next two wickets, putting herself in the lead. Victoria knelt beside the first stake, which had a capital H etched into the top. She returned to the field in time for her next turn, not surprised the croquet set belonged to the Halls.

After lining up her shot, Victoria's ball stopped a few inches short of the wicket, leaving it in the way of anyone getting through. Theodore approached her as she yielded the court.

"Did you move in recently?" He scanned the surrounding yards. "I don't remember anyone in the house before I left for school. Are your parents around?"

"They're sick today." Victoria stormed away.

Theodore followed her off the field.

"I hope they get better soon." He spun the mallet in his hands. "You know we won't win on our own."

"I already told her." Hannah joined them behind the starting wicket. "Your parents could beat us blindfolded. I bet they went on a croquet honeymoon."

"We should team up," said Theodore. "Young versus old."

"You'd turn on your own parents?" asked Victoria. "What kind of son are you?"

She regretted her words as soon as they came out of her mouth. Why was she so edgy? Especially when she was trying to make new friends.

"It's only a game," Theodore said with a nervous laugh. "Don't you want to win?"

Victoria hadn't meant to snap at him. He was trying to even the odds against the adults, but she'd nearly scared him away. Perhaps winning wouldn't be too bad if that's what the others wanted.

"What do you suggest?" she asked.

"I'll keep them away from the hoops," he said. "Hannah will help you finish the course and become the rover. Then you can knock my parents and Mr. Kennedy out of the game."

"Sounds like we'd be playing as a team," said Victoria. "Why the sudden change of heart?"

"What are you talking about?" Theodore planted the mallet on the ground. "I only said I didn't want to be on my parents' team like I have been since second grade."

"It's my turn." Hannah headed toward her ball. "I need to know what we're doing."

"It's not fair to change things after we started," said Victoria. "But go ahead and team up with him if you want."

Theodore curled his lips with a quick nod and returned to the field.

What was wrong with being on your parents' team every year? If he didn't want to spend time with them, he shouldn't have come back from school. Now he was on his own. Victoria hoped Hannah would understand, but if the two of them joined against her, she didn't care. She already knew what it felt like to be alone.

Hannah took a big swing, causing her ball to knock Victoria's ball through the third hoop. Victoria wasn't sure if she did it because she was blocking Hannah's or because her friend wanted to give her a boost. Either way, she was one hoop closer to finishing the course. She glanced at Hannah, but her friend just scowled back. The previous shot must have been an accident. Victoria couldn't have felt worse if she'd knocked Hannah out of the game. Hopefully, Hannah would forgive her by the end of the game.

Several turns passed, with the Halls sabotaging their chance to win as a family. One of them would hit another one's ball to the end of the field, only to have the gesture returned during the next round. Their behavior frustrated Victoria. Members of a family should always help one another, even if they're arguing. She squeezed the mallet and said nothing. Mr. Kennedy took advantage of the situation and stayed out of the fray, focusing on sending his ball through the remaining hoops.

Hannah avoided Victoria even after Victoria had helped her through a couple of wickets at the expense of her own progression. Why had she caused trouble between them? She could have joined the youngster's team and enjoyed the game. It would have been better if she'd stayed home and finished her homework, which was piling up on her dresser. Thankfully, the game would end soon, with Mr. Kennedy nearing the final stake.

There was little reason for Victoria to continue playing. Still trying to make it through the fourth hoop, last place would be hers. Hannah kept smiling during her turn, even though she couldn't win either. She seemed to have fun spending time with the neighbors, win or lose. Quitting now would only drive her friend further away. Victoria refused to imagine spending the rest of the year on her own at school. If Hannah could enjoy playing, so could she.

Mr. Kennedy finished the course first and became the rover on his next turn. He kept all three Halls scurrying around the course, while allowing Hannah and Victoria to send their balls through the hoops one at a time. Eventually, Hannah hit the final stake, followed by Victoria, Mr. and Mrs. Kennedy, and Theodore. They all shook hands and complimented one another on the game before returning to the food tables, but Victoria remained behind to help Hannah transfer the equipment to the next group of players. Theodore and his family could have won the game by sticking together but wound up in last place. Maybe they'd learn their lesson for next year, or maybe they only cared about having a good time together. They seemed happy.

"Looks like someone brought new goodies," said Hannah. "Wanna try some?"

"I'm going home to take care of my family," said Victoria. "Bring a few of the yummiest cookies on Monday."

"Sure." Hannah turned to the dessert table. "I hope they get better soon."

"Thanks. I'll let them know you're thinking of them."

Victoria headed up the street, where her house loomed with its shades drawn, hiding from the rest of the neighborhood. She wiped a tear from her eyes, hoping she could be on her parents' croquet team next year.

Chapter V

Opening Doors

Instead of an alarm beeping, a flash of lightning woke Victoria from her dreams. She rolled over, but rain pounded against her window, warning her not to fall back asleep. This wasn't a day to face reality. It was a day to hide from the world, no different from what the sun was doing. A loud rumble of thunder admonished the thought. Victoria dragged herself out of bed and threw on the nearest set of clothes. It no longer mattered if the top matched the bottom.

Downstairs, Victoria's mother had prepared the usual breakfast, filling the house with the invigorating scent of eggs and bacon. The brisk aroma of fresh coffee resting at her father's place setting almost convinced her to give this day a chance. Eli had already eaten his cereal, and Victoria's father remained buried in the newspaper, leaving his steaming mug untouched. There was no reason for her to eat alone in the kitchen. She brought her food into the living room and stared out of a crack between the shades. The gray clouds sucked all the color from the grass and trees, making it appear gloomier than the dead of winter. Even her food tasted bland, but she finished everything her mother had served.

"Is everything okay, dear?" Her mother removed the empty plate.

"Hannah's angry at me," Victoria said without looking up. "We might not be friends anymore. Why should I bother meeting anyone if they leave me after a few days?"

"If she's so quick to drop you, then you were never friends to begin with." Her mother brought the plate into the kitchen, pausing between the two rooms. "Talk to her. Apologize if you said something wrong. She'll forgive you."

"I wasn't nice to her on Saturday and haven't heard from her since."

Victoria grabbed her backpack and headed for the door, resolved to make amends with Hannah.

"Don't forget your umbrella," her mom called out. "It's buried in the closet."

"I didn't forget it." Victoria fished through a mound of clothes stuffed into the closet.

The coats barely budged, squeezed onto a wooden dowel. Most items had never been used in years, but Victoria couldn't get rid of anything. The perfect opportunity to wear a specific coat could come up tomorrow or the next day. The umbrella was tucked in the corner, past a trio of heavy winter coats that had seen their last snowfall. She brushed the furry top of a thick parka with her fingers, remembering the time when it tickled her neck on a ski lift in Vermont. Her toes had gone numb in her ski boots and her fingertips tingled in the cold, but she wanted to go down the mountain one more time. Against her father's advice, she and her mother went up the slope for one last run. It took her several hours to warm up afterwards, but the exhilaration of having the trails to themselves was worth the extra time spent in front of the fireplace.

"Don't dawdle," her mother said from the kitchen. "The bus will be here soon."

"I'm not dawdling." Victoria snatched the umbrella and left the house, arriving at the bus stop just in time to get on board.

Hannah wasn't in her usual seat. Perhaps she'd caught a cold and would be out sick for a couple of days. Victoria sank deeper into the seat, ignoring the continual pings and beeps of the nearby phones. She'd have to accept being alone until Hannah was feeling better. When the bus arrived at school, she shuffled outside without bothering to open the umbrella, getting soaked before reaching the safety of the main hallway.

As Victoria neared her locker, Brandon from the lunch table stared at her.

"What?" She shook her head, spraying water onto the hallway floor. "You've never seen a girl with wet hair?"

He turned away from both her and a chorus of giggles down the hall, but he still peeked in her direction. Boys.

Victoria ignored him while she spun the dial on her lock. He was probably planning a practical joke with his friends, maybe to sneak something into her locker to scare her the next time she opened it. Halloween was a couple of weeks away, but some people extended the holiday longer than it deserved–fake spiders in backpacks, nonstop discussions about the latest horror movies, and random screams from around corners. She didn't mind the treat portion of Halloween, but the tricks could be toned down. As she glanced over her shoulder, Brandon looked the other way.

"You're not getting into this locker," she said. "Find someone else to scare... and wait until Halloween's closer."

When the first bell rang, Brandon took off down the hallway.

"Yeah, you run," she called after him. "Tell your friends I'm not falling for your tricks."

She jammed her jacket and umbrella into her locker, forced the door to close, and rushed to her first class.

Hannah showed up in biology class halfway through third period. She dropped a note on the teacher's desk and quietly took her seat. Victoria glanced at her, but Hannah kept her head down. Was she still angry about not teaming up during the croquet game? At least she didn't seem to be sick. A sincere apology might set things right between them.

The teacher droned on about genes and natural selection for what felt like hours, but the dark clouds outside mesmerized Victoria. The sun might never show itself again. She didn't hear the lecture for the last twenty minutes and wouldn't have acknowledged the fire alarm if a drill had occurred during the period.

"Victoria." Her teacher clapped her hands. "Stop daydreaming and pick up your work."

Victoria looked on the floor around her desk, but none of her stuff had fallen off of her desk. Hannah pointed to the front, where the teacher held out a stack of papers. A few hushed chuckles followed Victoria to the desk as she collected her graded assignments. She kept her eyes on the floor as she returned to her seat, ignoring the whispers surrounding her. Why couldn't they leave her alone?

The teacher handed out papers until the bell rang, allowing Victoria to sift through her pile. Mixed in with old quizzes and homework was a thick packet of work to be finished by Monday. This was her life for the next several years. Sit through boring lectures by day and work on assignments at night, with a few hours set aside for eating and sleeping. After finishing high school and college, a tedious job would replace the lectures, while cooking and cleaning would replace the homework. Of course, all this tedium would eventually end in death. With a sigh, she headed for her locker. Did it matter if she made up with Hannah?

After confirming Brandon wasn't spying on her, Victoria unlocked the door, sending her umbrella and a stack of papers onto the ground.

"You really should clean that out," Hannah said on her way over. She bent down to pick up the fallen items. "It's only the first quarter and you've filled your allotted space. You can keep some things in my locker if you want—it's mostly empty."

"I wouldn't want to squeeze you out," said Victoria. "I could fill this entire row by the end of the year."

"No argument here." Hannah handed over the papers. "But I doubt Mr. Moritz would let you have them. He's not the most accommodating person."

"I thought you were mad at me."

"About what?"

Victoria shoved the papers into her locker along with her umbrella and the graded work she just received.

"For snapping at you during the game on Saturday."

"Oh, I already forgot about that. You were just upset that your family was sick."

A cloud lifted from Victoria's heart. Why was she worried about a single conversation? Her mom was right about Hannah, although the two hadn't met. A genuine friendship could withstand minor squabbles. The hall brightened as the sun forced itself through the clouds. This day wasn't so dreary, after all.

Hannah inched closer to the locker. "Are you sure you don't want help to straighten up a bit?"

"I'm not throwing anything away," said Victoria. "What if I need it for studying?"

"I didn't suggest getting rid of papers," said Hannah. "Take some back to your house. You don't need everything with you in school, like these notes about every chapter."

"I'll deal with it another day." Victoria slammed the door shut and spun the lock. "As long as this thing closes, I'm good."

"I give you to the end of the week." Hannah smiled at her. "If you're lucky."

"Why weren't you on the bus this morning?"

Hannah's bright demeanor faded a notch.

"It was nothing," she said. "Ready for gym?"

Victoria would have been upset at the curt answer, but she was keeping secrets from Hannah. She had to allow her friend a few of her own.

"Let's go," she said, "before we're stuck on opposite teams."

After making up with Hannah, gym and art quickly gave way to lunch. Victoria sped through the line and headed for her table, where Hannah had already unpacked her food.

"Mac and cheese again," said Victoria.

Hannah pushed Victoria's seat out for her "If you call that cheese."

"It's better than most of the meals here."

A foil-wrapped sandwich dominated Hannah's place setting, and a baggie of celery sticks sat nearby. At the end of the table, Brandon and his friends were unusually talkative, although they spoke in whispers to one another. If they were similar to the boys in middle school, they were thinking of ways to embarrass Victoria after failing at her locker. She glared at them before digging into her food. When would they grow up?

Although Hannah was correct about the sauce not being real cheese, it was creamy and had the right amount of tang. Did it matter if it was a processed cheese product instead of hand-crafted cheddar from an organic dairy farm? It tasted good to Victoria, much better than her side dish, soggy broccoli passing as a vegetable. Victoria tolerated it by combining the green chunks with her main course. Meanwhile, Hannah munched on her fresh vegetables, took a bite of her sandwich, and washed it all down with a swig of cold water.

"You can bring your own food if you don't like what they serve," said Hannah.

"That would mean more grocery shopping." Victoria forced down her last bite.

"Your mom won't mind." Hannah collected her garbage into her paper bag and rolled it into a ball. "Isn't she at the store twice a week? What's an extra loaf of bread and some fillings?"

"This wasn't so bad." Victoria finished her jar of pale juice. "And there's always pizza day."

She rose from the table and put Hannah's trash onto her plate. Brandon followed her to the dirty tray slot. Half the food was still on his plate, and he hadn't opened his milk carton. Victoria figured he wasn't hungry because he'd eaten a big breakfast. He shoved his tray through the slot, rushed to the door, and blocked her from exiting the cafeteria.

"Um..." He turned his head away.

She couldn't be sure, but he might have brushed his hair.

"Go find someone else to tease," she said. "I'm not in the mood."

"I'd never..." His eyes finally returned to her.

"What do you want?" Victoria sidestepped around him. "If I'm late for class again, I'll get a detention."

"I'm sorry... I don't want to cause any trouble." He followed her into the hallway.

Why couldn't he leave her alone?

"The freshman dance is next week," he blurted out. "Do you want to go?"

"To the dance?" Victoria stumbled as she spun around. "With you?"

He nodded, his cheeks turning bright red. Victoria hadn't thought about going to the dance, but she couldn't turn him down after being so mean. He'd ignored her nasty behavior and dug up the courage to ask her out. If she'd been in his place, a rejection would have devastated her.

A swath of dark hair covered part of his face, and his hands quivered. His hopeful look reminded Victoria of her desire to find new friends at the beginning of school. If she wasn't open to meeting new people, why should anyone else accept her?

"Sure," she said.

"Should I pick you up at seven?"

"How can you be driving already?"

"My dad will bring us to school," he said. "I'll make him promise not to say anything. Sometimes he can be embarrassing."

"I'd rather meet here," said Victoria. "Same time."

"Great. See you then." He took off in the opposite direction, jogging down the hallway to tell his friends about his success.

Victoria smiled. Maybe the dance wouldn't be bad.

After the bell rang, Victoria returned to her locker to swap some books she needed for homework. Hannah stood a few doors down in front of her open locker, which appeared as neat as her backpack. Every book had its own spot, while manila folders organized every piece of paper. A few boys, including Brandon, marched down the hallway toward the exit, talking about their plans for the afternoon.

What would Hannah think about Victoria going to the dance? She didn't want her friend to be jealous, but she didn't know if Hannah wanted to go. Should she bring up the subject or not say anything? Too many secrets would ruin their friendship. Too few might ruin her life. Hannah joined her at the locker.

"Brandon asked me to the dance," said Victoria. "I hope you don't mind."

"Why would I mind?" asked Hannah. "I'm not dating him."

"Do you want to come with us?"

"And be the odd one out on a date?" Hannah leaned against the row of lockers. "No thanks."

"It's not much of a date," said Victoria. "We're meeting at school, but I don't even want to dance. I don't know how."

"I can show up and teach you a few moves," said Hannah, "but I'm more interested in the school Halloween party. It's coming soon. Let's go as zombie sisters."

"I'd prefer something else." Victoria unlocked the door. "I'm not into the horror scene."

"Fine, I'll think of another costume, but promise we're going together."

Victoria opened her locker, causing another stack of papers to scatter in the hallway. As she bent over to pick them up, a shiny black shoe stepped in front of her face. She knew who it was without looking up.

"You may keep your locker as messy as you'd like," said Mr. Moritz, "but you may not litter the hallway, young lady."

"I'm sorry, sir." Victoria scooped up the papers. "I didn't mean for anything to fall out."

"I do not want a single pencil shaving on the floor," he said. "Am I clear?"

What did he want? To save money on janitorial service? Victoria nodded as she removed her umbrella and jacket, making it easier to close the locker. After the vice principal walked away to hassle other students, Hannah leaned in closer.

"You can always make this mess go away on its own," she whispered.

"What do you mean?"

"Like you made the garbage can move," said Hannah. "Have it run down the hallway and jump into the trash can? It'll clear your locker and freak out Mr. Moritz at the same time. He deserves a scare."

"I don't know what you're talking about."

Hannah gave her a sly grin and led her toward the bus.

"Well, if you ever figure it out," she said, "let me know."

Victoria wanted to reveal her secret to Hannah. It might strengthen their bond, but could she trust her friend not to tell anyone, including her parents? One wrong word and the entire town would be at her door asking questions. She couldn't take such a risk.

CHAPTER VI

THE FRESHMAN DANCE

After digging through boxes of clothing, Victoria hadn't found an acceptable outfit to wear to the dance. At some point, she'd have to unpack her belongings, but there was always something more important to complete. Between finishing her homework and setting the dinner table, she didn't have time to decide what to wear tonight. Many of her clothes didn't fit or were faded, but she uncovered a few possibilities. Eventually, she settled on a colorful dress her mom had worn to a beach party several years ago. It was loose in the waist, but Victoria pulled it tighter with a thin belt and accented the dress with a gold necklace.

Her mother was cleaning the kitchen, and her father was planted in front of the television watching the news. She would have stayed home for a quiet night with her family if she hadn't promised to meet Brandon at the dance. Why did he have to ask her? She tiptoed out of her room, but Eli must have heard her footsteps and rushed to intercept her.

"Where are you going?" he asked from the top of the stairs.

"I'm meeting someone at school." Victoria put on a light jacket.

"Is it a date?"

"Don't bother me or I'll be late," said Victoria.

"That means it's a date." Eli threw air kisses at her. "Who's the boy?"

"Just go back to your room and play your games."

"Fine," said Eli, "but I know the truth."

She avoided eye contact with him as she headed out.

The nearest transit bus stopped a few blocks from her house. Even if she could drive, she would have preferred to take public transportation. It was inexpensive, convenient, and safer than owning a car. Her legs wobbled when she thought about the dance, growing more nervous by the second. Maybe her father was right. She was too young for dating. Ignoring her fears, she boarded the bus and found a seat.

She considered remaining on the bus for a loop around town to calm herself, but Brandon would think she'd stood him up. Instead, she exited the bus down the street from school and trudged the short distance, pausing to adjust her dress.

Dozens of kids headed into the back building, some in pairs and others in large groups, but all wore fancy outfits. The boys had rented suits and ties, while the girls sported long gowns, most of them in dark colors. This was more formal than a casual dance, and Victoria felt under dressed in her plain outfit. She wanted to go home as soon as possible. Brandon would understand if she said hello and left. They'd never gone out before, so they didn't owe each other a specific amount of time together.

Brandon showed up a few minutes later, looking like he'd flee at the slightest sign of trouble. As bad as Victoria felt about her dress, he appeared far more uncomfortable. None of his friends from the lunch table had joined him. He glanced around the gym as if a predator was waiting to pounce on him from the shadows. A smile crossed his face when Victoria waved. He started toward her but was beaten by a cluster of popular girls led by Clare and Belle.

"Looks like you've given up trying to impress us," said Clare. "Where did you find that rag? At a nursing home tag sale?"

The other girls laughed, half of them flinging hair off their eyes. Instead of angering Victoria, the teasing validated her choice of clothing. These girls proved they had no thoughts of their own, each one copying the other. Victoria wouldn't have been surprised if Clare and Belle had stolen a look they saw in some teen magazine. Didn't they know those fashions were created only to make money? Thankfully, things didn't work out between her and the popular girls. She would have been miserable following them around and pretending to be someone else.

Belle took the sleeve of Victoria's dress between her thumb and index finger.

"Polyester," she said. "I bet her mother wore it decades ago."

Victoria yanked her arm away. "Don't touch me."

"It must have been her mother's," said Clare. "Did she wear it to her first dance?"

"Don't talk about my mother." Victoria sneered at them. "My date's here. Some of us didn't come to the dance alone."

She stepped around the group and approached Brandon, but the girls weren't done with her yet. They surrounded Victoria and Brandon, leaving no room for escape.

"If you two are together," said Clare, "let's see you dance."

Brandon's face turned bright red as he looked for a way to break from the pack, but the girls closed off any possible escape. It must have taken all his courage to ask Victoria out, and he didn't appear to have anything left.

"Since you came to the dance together," said Victoria, "why don't you start? We'll join in if we're not embarrassed by your lame moves."

Half the girls looked at one another, clearly against any form of motion other than skulking around the gym in a pack. Clare would lose most of the group if she persisted. She led her friends away.

"Have fun standing there awkwardly," Clare called out over her shoulder.

Brandon took Victoria aside. "Aren't you afraid they'll make your life miserable at school?"

"There's nothing they can do to me," said Victoria. "I've already seen the worst."

"Oh, no. Did they hurt you?" Brandon stepped backward to look at her. "What happened?"

"Nothing I want to talk about," said Victoria. "Do you mind if I leave now?"

"Because I didn't stand up to them?"

"Because they were right. I'm not dressed for a formal."

"But you look beautiful," said Brandon.

"Thanks." One more compliment and Victoria's cheeks would be the same color as his. "I guess I can stay a bit longer. Let's get something to drink."

She led him to the corner of the gym, where a large punch bowl sat on a table with a stack of plastic cups nearby. When they both grabbed the ladle, Victoria yanked her hand back. Her fingers caught the stem of the ladle and sent a splash of pink juice everywhere, including her dress. She and Brandon each grabbed a stack of napkins and started cleaning the mess before anyone noticed. After rushing to dry the floor, he continued wiping the juice from her shoe and up her leg.

Victoria jumped backward. "What are you doing?"

"I'm sorry." Brandon dropped the napkin and held his hands away. "I was cleaning the last of the punch. I didn't mean to —"

"I'll be right back." Victoria headed toward the girls' locker room.

Behind her, Brandon poured two cups of punch and drifted toward the bleachers, away from the crowd. He claimed he was innocent, but he was quick to touch her body under the guise of cleaning the spill. She had to keep her guard up.

In the bathroom, the stain came out with a dab of water, but the lighting wasn't good enough to see clearly. Victoria hoped the material wasn't ruined, although nothing would diminish her memory of this dress at the beach party. Her mother looked like a brilliant sapphire against the sand, far more beautiful than any other guest.

Clare and her cluster of cronies blocked Victoria on her way out of the locker room.

"Bored with Brandon already?" asked Clare. "I don't blame you. I almost fell asleep looking at him."

A few giggles punctuated the statement, bringing a grin to her face. Victoria wasn't interested in more drama, but they refused to let her pass. She glanced at their high heels, most of the girls doing their best to stand upright. A simple gesture would put their shoes under her control and send them all to the ground, but at least one of them would become suspicious. She couldn't rely on her special power.

"Or you're jealous that none of you are on a date." Victoria returned her smirk.

"We all have dates," said Belle. "We're just—"

"Hanging out together because you're bored with your guys." Victoria winked at her. "No need to explain. I understand. Anyone asking you out would have to be devoid of personality."

Clare and Belle moved closer, followed by the rest of the group. They seemed to be done talking. Victoria's heart raced. If they tried anything physical, she'd turn their own clothing against them. Too bad it wasn't in the middle of the party, where they'd be embarrassed when their dresses gained minds of their own.

"Why don't you ladies return to the dance floor," said a chaperone making her rounds. "I doubt you need everyone in a group to use the bathroom."

A few girls bumped into Victoria on their way out of the locker room. Victoria returned to the gym and found Brandon off to the side. He'd finished his drink but still held hers, which he offered upon her arrival. Victoria took a tentative sip while watching the pack of popular girls hover near the dance floor without moving to the music. They didn't deserve to be the center of attention, unless there was a reason to draw eyes toward them.

Victoria felt a hand on her shoulder, causing her to jerk backward.

"Sorry to startle you." Brandon pulled away from her. "I was asking if you wanted to dance."

"I still have my drink," said Victoria.

He appeared to understand, but this excuse wouldn't last long. She couldn't ignore him for the entire night after accepting his invitation, but she was too self-conscious to dance. A few couples swayed to the music, but more kids were hanging around chatting. Perhaps they'd ignore her if she and Brandon joined the festivities, although the popular girls would jump at any chance to resume their teasing. A quick glance confirmed none of them were looking in her direction—probably waiting for her to become more vulnerable.

"Maybe we shouldn't have come tonight," said Brandon. "You don't seem comfortable."

"Why does everyone like them? They're just mean."

"Not everyone likes them." Brandon positioned himself between Victoria and the popular gang. "Only the boys who find them attractive and the girls who want to be part of their group, and I bet 'like' is pushing it."

"Yeah." Victoria tossed her cup in the nearest trash can. "I'll forget about them. The deejay's playing a decent song. We might as well give it a shot."

Brandon led her to the center of the gym, giving the popular girls a wide berth. Victoria felt hundreds of eyes on her, but a scan of the dance floor proved no one cared. Clare and her gang were chatting with Lou and Mike, who clearly didn't want to dance.

The music blared, with the amps directed at the center of the gym. Although the tempo was upbeat, it didn't inspire Victoria to dance. Around her, kids and chaperones were jumping up and down, waving their arms, and shaking their bodies. If she tried any dance moves, she'd prove she didn't belong among them, but standing still amid the constant gyrations wasn't any better.

Brandon shimmied to the beat with his arms in the air, smiling at her. Did he realize she wasn't dancing, or didn't he care? She tapped her foot in sync with a popular song that had been playing on the radio every few hours, but just when she was ready to loosen up, the deejay announced a request from Clare and changed the track to a slow song.

"Should we go back to the bleachers?" asked Brandon.

Victoria eyed Clare within her pack of friends. "Keep dancing."

She couldn't let them win. Brandon took her hand in his and placed his other hand on her back, pulling her closer. Victoria rested her free arm on his shoulder and swayed to the music.

"Clare thought her gang could scare me away," said Victoria. "I can't believe I wanted to become part of their group. What I was thinking?"

"Forget about them. They don't care if you have fun," Brandon said as he accidentally stepped on her foot. "Sorry."

He turned Victoria so her back was to the popular girls, but Victoria still felt their eyes resting on her. They wanted to prove she didn't belong here, but she wouldn't give them the satisfaction, especially since she had a date and they didn't. Although it was awkward with Brandon, she wasn't about to leave.

While they danced, Brandon knocked into her twice and stepped on her foot once more. She wasn't surprised he didn't know how to dance, but his clumsiness almost caused her to trip each time. Clare and the others would never let her forget this night if she embarrassed herself. She squeezed Brandon's hand and pushed him sideways.

"You're supposed to let me lead," said Brandon.

"I'm not used to this, but I'm pretty sure you're not supposed to kick me."

"I said I was sorry."

He turned her around again, but his foot caught against her leg, causing her to lose her balance. As she fell, he clutched her dress and pulled it off her shoulders. Everyone in the gym would be staring at her within seconds, including the popular girls, who'd waste no time making her life miserable.

With seconds to find a better target for their attention, Victoria focused on Brandon's jacket and imbued it with life. The living jacket climbed up his back to free itself from his body. Brandon tore the thing off and threw it onto the floor.

"A rat!" His scream set off a bunch of shrieks from the surrounding students.

Victoria regretted animating something so close to her, but she didn't have the leisure to come up with a better plan. Now she couldn't let anyone see the jacket moving on its own. She raised her hand again, stared at the nearest fire alarm, and allowed it to set itself off. The alarm blasted throughout the building, drowning out the music and sending the gym into chaos.

Students rushed to the exits, more disorganized than any drill Victoria had taken part in during school. Nearby, Brandon's jacket crawled away from the confusion. It would remain alive for several minutes if she did nothing. Unwilling to risk anyone noticing the strange creature, Victoria pounced on the jacket, returned it to normal, and handed it to Brandon.

"The rat must have run off in the chaos." She fixed her dress.

Brandon helped her off the floor and escorted her outside, where students and teachers waited for the fire department. Half the kids were calling for rides home, while the others continued their conversations in the new venue. They didn't care if the school burned down.

"I wonder who set off the alarm." Brandon gazed at the building.

"I was too distracted to see anything," said Victoria. "I should go home now."

"Do you want me to walk with you?"

"I'll be fine." Victoria turned toward the bus stop. "Thanks, anyway."

"I'm sorry about the dancing," said Brandon. "I didn't mean to pull your dress. It was an accident."

"Sure, but let's just keep this to ourselves." Victoria strolled away, hoping to forget about the night. "See you Monday."

Chapter VII

Halloween

Hannah stared at Victoria from the moment she stepped on the bus. Victoria checked to see if her shirt was unbuttoned, but it looked fine. Her pants matched the top and were mostly clean. Did she forget to brush her hair? Monday mornings were more difficult than the rest of the week, but she'd gone to bed early enough for a good night's sleep.

"What?" she asked as she sat beside her friend.

"I heard there was excitement at the dance," said Hannah. "You didn't want to mention anything sooner? The dance was two and a half days ago."

"How did you hear about it?" Victoria edged away from her until she hung off the seat. "I didn't think you had any other friends who were there Friday."

Hannah turned to her and scooted closer.

"I saw pictures online," she said. "It must have been wild."

"What pictures?" Victoria became worried there was proof of her misdeeds.

At least Hannah didn't say there were videos of a jacket moving on its own. A picture was easier to fake, giving Victoria an alternate explanation of the events if necessary. She held her breath and prepared an excuse.

"Everyone was waiting in the dark while the fire department checked the building." Hannah showed her a social media feed with several pictures of freshmen standing outside the gym. "Lucky it didn't rain."

"I went home by then." Victoria's muscles relaxed. "Things didn't work out with Brandon."

"Sorry you didn't enjoy the date," said Hannah. "He seemed decent. It's strange that people heard shouts about a rat before the alarm went off. Or was it a squirrel?"

"Probably a crazy kid who wanted to cause confusion."

"And I stayed home because I thought it would be another boring dance."

Hannah grabbed her lunch bag.

"I came up with an idea for our costumes." She took out a foil-wrapped sandwich to show Victoria. "What do you think?"

"Looks yummy." Victoria was relieved that her friend had changed the subject. "What does your lunch have to do with Halloween?"

"We're going as a peanut butter and jelly sandwich."

Halloween arrived with a brisk change in the weather. Mild days had given way to chilly breezes, and comfortable nights required thicker coats. The kids at school never talked about trick-or-treating, but most of them were excited to dress up for the big party. Even teachers and administrators were preparing for the Halloween Gala, the largest party of the year. Some people spent months creating their costumes. Although she wouldn't have gone if Hannah hadn't invited her, Victoria wanted to see her teachers dressed up.

She pulled a brown foam square over her shirt and stuck her arms through holes in the sides. Hannah had done a great job sewing the outfit over the past few days. Each afternoon, she'd rushed home from school and ignored her homework to create the perfect replica of a slice of bread slathered with peanut butter. The complementary piece was sure to be incredible. Victoria had done her part by picking up brown leggings for herself and purple ones for Hannah, but any award would go to her friend. The prize for best costume was a sizable gift certificate to the local crafts store, giving the winner a head start on next year's entry.

Downstairs, Victoria's parents had put up cardboard ghosts and filled a large basket with bags of candy. Victoria didn't bother decorating her room. Boxes of clothing still covered her floor, more cluttered than ever. As long as everything was there, did it matter if it was organized? She'd find a shirt to wear if it was stuffed in a drawer, hanging in the closet, or packed in a cardboard moving box.

Eli remained in his bedroom with the door closed, upset he wasn't allowed to go out until they learned more about the neighborhood. He'd get over it when he was stuffing his mouth with the extra candy they didn't hand out. Besides, with incessant video game beeps coming through the wall, he couldn't have been too distraught.

The doorbell rang before Victoria finished brushing her hair. She glanced outside. It was too light for kids to be collecting candy yet, and she wasn't expecting any guests.

"I'll get it." She bolted downstairs.

Her mother had already opened the door, and her father was a few steps away. Victoria charged forward to find Hannah standing at the threshold in her jelly costume. Feet shuffled upstairs. Eli was on his way down. He never could resist candy. Victoria inserted herself between her friend and her mother.

"Now I see why you didn't want to go as zombie sisters," said Hannah. "Your parents dressed like zombies this year. I love the costume Mrs.—"

"We were supposed to meet at your house," said Victoria. "Why did you change our plans?"

"I haven't gone trick-or-treating in years." Hannah pressed forward to come inside. "I figured I could pick up snacks on the way over—in case we get hungry walking to school."

She displayed an assortment of bite-sized candies in her palms. With only a couple of houses between hers and Victoria's, she probably went up and down the street before coming over. If she wanted more candy, she should have told Victoria. They could have gone door-to-door together.

"Those look delicious." Victoria's mother squeezed onto the threshold beside Victoria. "You must be Hannah. I've heard so much about you."

"It's nice to meet you."

Hannah shoved the candies into one hand and held out the other to shake, but Victoria pushed her back outside.

"We should get going," said Victoria. "I don't want to be late."

"It's still early," said her mother. "The party won't end before ten or eleven. Why don't you come in and visit? We rarely entertain guests these days."

Hannah peered around Victoria into the house.

"Who's that?" she asked.

Eli peeked from the doorway.

"That's my annoying brother, Eli." Victoria moved in front of him. "He's being home schooled."

"And in the two months since we met, you didn't mention a sibling?" Hannah frowned at her with jaws clenched. "Anyone else you're not telling me about? A cute older brother?"

"Just Eli." Victoria tugged at Hannah's costume. "Can we go now?"

Eli stepped outside with them and gazed into the sky. "I want to go with you."

"The party's just for high school students," said Victoria. "Go back inside."

"Aw, let him come with us." Hannah waved him forward. "I'm sure other people are bringing guests. You never told me how much your family is into Halloween."

"Yeah, we all love it."

"I wish I was your sister," said Hannah. "My mom is against every part of this holiday. She called it a pagan tradition that should have faded away long ago."

"But she let you make these wonderful costumes." Victoria ushered Eli back into the house. "She can't be too against it."

"I had to take on an extra chore for the next three months." Hannah curtsied. "You're looking at the new laundry maid."

"Sorry about that." Victoria headed for the walkway.

"Why are you against bringing Eli?" asked Hannah.

"He already has an evening of fun planned."

"I'm going trick-or-treating?" His lips curled into a smile. "When?"

"Not today." Victoria faced her brother but kept her gaze on the front steps. "You're keeping track of all the costumes for me. Take pictures of the best ones. Also, there's a bunch of candy to hand out, and you get to eat anything that's left over."

"Really?"

Eli danced down the hallway toward the basket of candy, probably to pick out which pieces he'd hide for himself.

"Don't come home late," said Victoria's mother. "We still don't know about these neighborhoods after dark."

"Don't worry," said Hannah. "It'll be quiet around here by seven, and if any wild kids are roaming closer to the school, we'll call for a ride. My mom's not doing anything tonight."

"Or we can take the bus," said Victoria. "I brought enough change for both of us."

The Halloween Gala had taken over the gym and most of the main building. Fake cobwebs and skeletons hung from hallway ceilings, classrooms had been decorated in styles ranging from pirate ships to haunted houses, and students randomly jumped out of nooks to scare any passersby. None of the decorations had been present at school on Friday, so dozens of people must have spent the past two days setting up. Maybe the detailed work had counted for art class.

Victoria and Hannah roamed through the hallways, comparing the quality of the decorations to their own costumes. Other than a few standouts, Hannah claimed they'd win for best outfits. Victoria was skeptical. The overriding themes in the school were horror, hit television shows, and movies. Posing as a sandwich, even though they wore perfectly matched outfits, was unlikely to draw votes.

They ambled past several rooms but slowed when they came to their Spanish classroom, which had been converted into a graveyard, complete with fake grass and tombstones. Colorful masks lined the walls, providing a stark contrast to the dismal grays and browns in the rest of the room.

"Let's see what they wrote on the gravestones," said Hannah. "I bet some of them are funny."

"There's nothing to eat around here," Victoria said without stopping. "I'd rather look for some food in the gym."

"This won't take long." Hannah stepped inside. "It's a small room. Look, this one says, '*Yo debería volver*.' Do you think it means he'll return to Spanish class or back from the dead?"

Victoria returned to the doorway but didn't enter the classroom.

"I don't know." She scanned the grim decorations. "Does it matter?"

Hannah weaved around the desks, each one covered in old rags and spider webs, reading the messages. She screamed when someone roared from the back of the room. Victoria shook her head at the lame attempt at horror. Loud noises weren't scary; they were surprising—a big difference.

The boy who'd startled Hannah was an upperclassman dressed in torn clothing and covered in scars and fake blood. Enough with the zombies already. Victoria stepped away from the door and leaned against the wall. She shouldn't have come at all. Hannah could have found someone else to complete her costume.

In the room, Hannah talked to the boy about his makeup, no doubt gathering notes for next year's costume. They should go to the party together as matching undead. Victoria would never dress as a zombie.

"There you are." Hannah exited the room, smiling. "Did he scare you away?"

"I'm not into the whole living dead thing," said Victoria. "What's the point?"

"Right. Your family killed that genre when they dressed that way this year." Hannah took Victoria by the hand. "Let's peek into more rooms. We still have a good chance of winning the costume contest. People prefer to vote for group projects rather than individuals."

"Do we have to enter the contest?" asked Victoria. "Can't we just enjoy the party and goof on the lame outfits? We'll have more fun."

"Fine, but only because I spent less than a week making these," said Hannah. "The three months of chores were a bit of an exaggeration. Next year will be different, and you're gonna help. We can plan during summer break."

"That's a long way out," said Victoria. "I can barely figure out what I'll be doing next week."

She didn't know if she'd be living in the same town next year. People's situations could change in an instant, making it impossible to think about long-range plans. It would be terrible to lose Hannah as a friend, but she couldn't predict what might happen in life. Victoria shook her head to clear it of negative thoughts. Of course, they'd work on costumes together next summer. They were best friends.

The gym was no less decorated than the rest of the school. Orange and black streamers bridged the gaps between scoreboards and basketball nets; posters of bats, witches, and ghouls covered the walls; and jack-o'-lanterns sat in the bleachers, shining flickering lights out of their eyes and mouths. More than half the school was in attendance.

Scores of people were jammed between a dozen long tables, which displayed every type of treat imaginable. Victoria's mouth watered at the sight. She could choose a plate of monster-themed cookies, a heaping slice of pumpkin pie, or a handful of chocolates. Maybe a little of each would be best.

Costumes ranged from simple masks covering nothing but the eyes to full body suits with fur, claws, and tails. One boy sported a set of wings that folded in and out when he moved his arms. No matter how much anyone enjoyed the classic peanut butter and jelly sandwich, no one would vote for Hannah's costume. Victoria was happy they weren't competing anymore. She was about to discuss who they'd vote for when she spotted the popular girls in the corner.

Clare, Belle, and the rest of their flock had each dressed in a skimpy outfit. A couple of them wore cat ears on their heads, but most of them didn't have a point to their minimal costumes except showing as much skin as possible. Victoria ushered Hannah in the other direction, but not before Clare glimpsed their costumes and laughed. She led her mob toward Victoria.

"Shouldn't you be trick-or-treating with the rest of the kiddies?" asked Belle.

Victoria backed away, but several girls had positioned themselves behind her, forming a solid line of spectators.

"Did your mom make those outfits for you when you were five?" asked Clare. "You must have been fat kids for them to still fit."

The comments devastated Hannah, who seemed ready to burst into tears. It would have been worse if she'd worked on the costumes since the summer, but Victoria couldn't let the mean girls get away with nasty remarks. They could say what they wanted about her, but not her friend.

"Why are you always so cruel?" asked Victoria.

"I wasn't being mean." Clare batted her eyes at a passing boy. "I was only stating the obvious. Does anyone disagree?"

Blank stares answered her question, like any of them would have said something.

"I'd be surprised if you got a single vote," said Clare, "including your own."

She left with a smirk, bringing her gang to the refreshments table, where they poured an orange liquid into paper cups with a large ladle.

As soon as Hannah turned around, Victoria focused on the drinks, lifting her hand just enough to connect with the ladle. When it was Clare's turn to pour her drink, the ladle flipped over in her hand, splashing her with the punch. Splotches of orange soaked her dress from her shoulders down to the frilly hem.

"What happened?" Clare hopped away from the table, shocked at the mess.

Everyone stared at her, a few of them gasping. The noise drew Hannah's attention.

She returned the laughter the other girls had just doled out. "Drink much?"

Victoria rushed forward, snatched the ladle from Clare's grasp, and placed it back in the punch bowl before anyone could see its tiny legs. While the other girls fumbled with napkins, Clare turned to her.

"What did you do to the ladle?" she asked.

Victoria's gaze switched between Clare and the punch bowl. Had she noticed the ladle was alive? Victoria never should have used her ability, but she couldn't help herself. Now her secret might be out and ruin her life.

"We were way over there the whole time." Hannah joined them at the table. "Ask anyone in the room."

Victoria handed Clare a stack of napkins. "Face it, you're just clumsy."

Clare knocked the napkins out of Victoria's hand with a muted growl.

"And you're just a wannabe who'll never fit in." She grabbed ice cubes from a nearby bowl. "Go hang out with your sandwich buddy someplace else."

Hannah nudged Victoria toward the door, still giggling.

"This party's no fun," she said. "Let's go to my house."

Victoria followed her out of the gym, wondering what had changed Hannah's mind so drastically.

CHAPTER VIII

ANIMATED LIFE

As Victoria and Hannah exited the gym, a boy in a furry dog costume chased after them. The dog's head was nearly the same size as the rest of the costume, with floppy ears, a long snout, and big brown eyes. It belonged in a theme park more than on a teenager during Halloween.

"Why are you leaving?" The heavy mask covering his head muffled his voice. "It's still early."

"Brandon?" said Victoria. "Is that you?"

Brandon lifted the mask off his shoulders and held it under his arm. "How did you guess?"

"No one else would care whether I stayed or left," said Victoria. "Did you see what happened in there?"

"Nah, but I heard laughs and saw people cleaning the spill. It doesn't look like you got wet this time. Why are you leaving? We can get punch after they bring out a fresh bowl."

Hannah had backed away to give them privacy, but Victoria wished she hadn't. Their costumes only made sense together. Without Hannah, she was half a sandwich, talking to a headless dog. She glanced around to make sure the popular girls hadn't followed them out. This sight would have been enough to make them forget a wet dress.

Brandon fiddled with the dog ears as he waited for Victoria's answer. Even if she'd come to the party on her own, she didn't want to be alone with a boy who wanted to date her, no matter how nice he was. Why did she have to grow up so quickly?

When girls from her old middle school started dating, Victoria's mother told her not to worry. Everyone matured at a different rate, and she'd know when it was her time. Now wasn't it, and she owed him an explanation.

"I don't want to date anyone yet." She hoped he wouldn't take it too hard.

"You don't?" A wave of relief seemed to pass through his body. "The other kids pressured me to ask you out. I thought they'd leave me alone after the dance, but it only got worse. Can we be friends?"

"Sure." Victoria waved Hannah back. "I've had enough of the party. See you tomorrow."

Brandon put the head back on his costume and jogged inside, his tail wagging with each step.

"What was that about?" Hannah led Victoria down the street.

"We agreed to be friends," said Victoria.

"So you don't think he and his pals are planning a practical joke against you?" Hannah gave her half a smile. "Not everyone in the school is mean."

"I know."

On their way home, Victoria and Hannah passed several groups of kids going door-to-door for candy, including some they recognized from school. Evidently, being in high school didn't mean you were too old for Halloween fun. Victoria wanted to join them at a few houses along the way, but Hannah kept ushering her down the sidewalk, increasing her pace as they went.

"What's going on?" Victoria had to jog to keep up with her. "We left the party early. There's no rush to get home. Besides, I thought you wanted extra candy."

Hannah stopped when they reached a part of the block with no one else around.

"You spilled the drink on Clare," she said in a hushed voice. "How did you do it?"

"Do what?" asked Victoria. "We were together the whole time, ten feet from the table."

"Really? I didn't notice."

"What do you think happened?" Victoria dreaded the response. She wasn't ready for everyone to know about her ability.

"You lifted your palm right before the spill." Hannah repeated the motion. "It was the same when we first met, but I stopped you. You were going to do something to Clare for embarrassing you in front of her friends."

Victoria had always known Hannah was observant, but she couldn't allow Clare and the others to get away with their hurtful remarks. She had to teach them a lesson, which now forced her to lie.

"You mean like this?" Victoria lifted one hand with her palm up, hoping to convince Hannah of her innocence. "It's nothing. See?"

She waved her hand and spun around in place. Hannah didn't move, still waiting for an explanation. Victoria raised her other hand into the air and wiggled her fingers. A few kids down the street noticed her and waved back.

"Fine." Hannah pulled Victoria's arms down. "Don't tell me anything. Confide in your new friend, Brandon. I won't stand here while you mock me. Something happened back there... I know it."

She marched away.

Victoria wanted to rush after her and tell the truth, but Hannah would treat her differently. Even if her friend didn't tell anyone, she'd become scared of Victoria—or jealous.

Several years ago, Victoria had a close friend whose family was wealthier than hers. They'd play together after school and have sleepovers every few months. As Victoria grew older, she kept asking her parents why they didn't have everything her friend had—a gigantic television, a gym in the basement, and a housekeeper to clean the rooms. Eventually, her parents became tired of her complaints and stopped letting them hang out together. Victoria didn't realize how jealous she'd become until her father yelled at her to stop comparing the two families. She never wanted Hannah to go through a similar ordeal.

Two blocks away, Hannah tripped on the curb and flew forward onto the ground. Victoria rushed over to find Hannah's legging ripped and her knee bleeding.

"That was a nasty fall." She offered a hand. "Are you okay?"

Hannah grabbed her arm and stood with difficulty. "I twisted my ankle."

"Here." Victoria put Hannah's arm around her shoulder. "I'll walk you home."

Now they truly looked like a peanut butter and jelly sandwich, squished together as they shuffled down the street.

"We should stop at your house," said Hannah. "It's closer."

"You'll be fine," said Victoria. "Your house is only a few steps more. We're almost there."

She supported Hannah's weight until they reached her friend's house. The lights were off, forcing the trick-or-treaters to skip Hannah's door, but no toilet paper hung from the trees in the front yard. No other walkways on this side of the block were dark. Perhaps the kids received enough candy to ignore the one holdout. In Victoria's old neighborhood, frustrated tricksters would clearly mark any house not taking part in the festivities.

"Is anybody home?" asked Victoria. "Your house looks dark."

"My mom should be there, otherwise we'll be stuck outside. This costume has no pockets. I left my keys in my room."

Hannah limped to the front door and rang the bell. No one answered. She pushed the button a second time and pounded on the door until her mother came.

"I wasn't expecting you home so early," she said. "What happened to your knee?"

"It's just a scrape," said Hannah. "Can Victoria come in?"

"Of course." Her mother helped her onto the living room sofa.

Victoria plopped down in a comfortable chair across from her friend.

Hannah rubbed her leg. "My ankle's a little better."

"Why wouldn't it be?" asked Victoria. "You're sitting down."

An upright piano stood in the corner and family photos adorned the walls. A small television faced the sofa with a black and white movie playing. Victoria didn't recognize the actors and the volume was off, but one character fell off a horse while riding.

Hannah's mother returned with a wet washcloth, a roll of gauze, and some tape. She cleaned Hannah's knee and covered the wound.

"Should I call the doctor?" she asked. "It doesn't look bad, but we should find out if it's sprained."

Hannah stood slowly, favoring her other leg.

"I'll see how it feels tomorrow." She hobbled to the staircase. "Let's go upstairs."

The house was laid out exactly like Victoria's, with the same number of rooms in the same spots. Victoria could have closed her eyes and navigated from one end to the other without knocking into a single wall. Hannah had the same bedroom as Victoria at the top of the stairs. Instead of a little brother occupying the room next door, however, Hannah's mother kept a home office, complete with a desk, a filing cabinet, and a computer. At the end of the hall was the master bedroom, where Hannah's parents slept. A shiver overcame Victoria. They should raise the thermostat a few degrees.

"It's the same as your house," said Hannah. "Nothing interesting down there. Are you coming in?"

Victoria followed her into the bedroom and closed the door. Nothing was out of place. Flowery sheets covered the bed, no clothing cluttered the floor or dresser top, and every book had its own space in the bookcase. A large bean bag chair lay in the corner beside a standing lamp, probably where Hannah did her reading.

A single picture hung on the wall above the desk. A cheery man in a baseball cap held a young girl in his arms. The girl had to be Hannah, sporting the same bright smile and long black hair. Victoria gravitated toward the photograph.

"We were in the park," said Hannah. "It was early spring and the snow had just melted. The ground was soggy, and I complained about getting my shoes wet. My dad picked me up, spun me around, and carried me to the picnic table. I don't remember what we ate or where we went after lunch, but I'll never forget his mud-encrusted shoes sitting in the hallway that night."

She hadn't mentioned her father once since they'd met, but they seemed to have a close relationship.

"Where is your dad?" Victoria wasn't sure she wanted to hear the answer. Why did she ask?

"He died two years ago." Hannah sat on the edge of her bed, gazing at the picture.

Victoria's legs gave out, sending her onto the bed next to her friend. Although she'd never met the man, she struggled to hold back tears.

"Pancreatic cancer," said Hannah. "One day he was fine, playing basketball with me in the driveway, and the next day he had a stomachache. He thought it was something he ate, but when it didn't go away after a week, he saw a doctor and got the bad news. A few months later..."

"I'm so sorry," said Victoria. "That's horrible. I can imagine how you felt."

"No, you can't." Hannah pulled her pillow into her lap. "You still have your family."

Losing a parent was devastating, enough to change one's view about life. Victoria would have done anything to protect her family, even if they annoyed her occasionally. Hannah had been powerless as she watched her father pass away. Victoria turned around to hide her watering eyes.

Hannah scooted up the bed to rest against the headboard.

"That's why I was late for school a few days ago," she said. "I couldn't cope with another dreary morning. My mom had to call the therapist."

"You go to therapy?"

"More than a year of sessions," said Hannah, "but I stopped several months ago when I seemed to be improving."

"That makes our vice principal even meaner than I thought." Victoria swung her legs onto the bed to face Hannah. "He knew you'd suffered a terrible loss and still harassed you about detention. What a jerk."

"It's not his fault," said Hannah. "I was acting out last year—yelling at other kids, calling them names, ignoring my teachers. Mr. Moritz was forgiving at first, but the therapist told him to stop treating me differently from everyone else."

Victoria stifled a chuckle.

"What's so funny?" Hannah asked with a frown.

"I'm trying to imagine you causing trouble," said Victoria. "It's hard to believe you'd do any of those things. You don't allow a speck of dust in your locker."

Hannah's face softened. Victoria hadn't forced her friend to talk about anything she wanted to keep private, yet Hannah's personal troubles had come out. She should have told her the truth from the beginning. Victoria felt a closer connection to Hannah than ever before.

She glanced at the beanbag chair in the corner. After Hannah's honesty about her father, Victoria couldn't keep her secret to herself. She concentrated on the chair and raised her palm upwards. Four legs sprouted from the bottom of the beanbag, which rose from its corner nook and ambled toward the bed.

"I knew it!" Hannah winced when she put pressure on her bandaged knee. "It was you at the party and with the garbage cans."

"Please don't tell anyone," said Victoria. "They'll think I'm a freak."

"I'd never let your secret out." Hannah inched forward. "This is amazing! How do you do it?"

"I don't know." Victoria patted that chair. "I just can."

Hannah hovered near the edge of the bed, staring at the creature.

"You can touch it," said Victoria. "It won't hurt you."

"Are you controlling it?"

Hannah reached out and stroked the top of the beanbag.

"Not really." Victoria moved from the bed onto the chair for a brief ride. "It's alive and can think for itself, but it knows it's connected to me. It might even know I gave it life, which is why it tries to please me."

"Will I have to feed it?"

The chair pranced around the room and deposited Victoria back on the bed.

"I can only keep it animated for a few minutes. If you want a ride, better make it quick."

"That's so sad," said Hannah. "What happens after?"

"It goes back to being a bean bag chair. I like to think it's just as happy being its normal self."

Hannah hesitated before climbing onto the chair. It shuffled her around the room several times, bumping into the furniture on each pass, before reverting to normal.

"Everything okay up there?" Hannah's mom shouted from downstairs. "You're making a lot of noise."

"Sorry, we'll be quieter." Hannah turned to Victoria. "Can you do it again?"

"Once more," said Victoria, "but then I'll need to rest. It takes a lot to animate larger items."

She concentrated on the chair, imbuing it with temporary life once more. The chair trotted around the room carrying Hannah. It seemed proud of its accomplishment, although it might have sensed Victoria's satisfaction of opening up to her friend.

"Have you always been able to do this?" Hannah returned to the bed.

"I'm not sure when it started," Victoria said with a yawn. "I should go now. Animating the chair was tiring. You don't have to see me out."

"You can trust me." Hannah gave her a firm hug and sank back into her pillow. "Not a word."

"I wouldn't have shown you otherwise. I hope your leg feels better tomorrow."

Victoria let herself out and headed home. For once, she was excited to go back to school. After strengthening her bond with Hannah, she didn't care how mean the popular girls were. She and Hannah would get through the teasing together. Nothing could break apart their friendship, as long as Victoria did nothing to scare her.

Chapter IX

The Trouble with Secrets

It wouldn't have surprised Victoria if Hannah wasn't on the bus. With a sore ankle, her friend might need a doctor's visit, but Hannah was waiting with a broad smile. Victoria swung her backpack onto her lap as she sat. With a thin jacket over her shirt, the extra nip in the air didn't bother her.

"How's the injury?" she asked.

Hannah hiked up her legging to display a swollen ankle and a bloody gauze pad on her knee.

"Not bad." She fixed her clothing. "We already called the doctor. He said to ice my ankle for a couple of days and schedule an appointment if it doesn't improve."

"At least you get out of gym," said Victoria. "We're stuck with the worst of the freshman class. Having gym any other period would have been better."

"It won't be all fun for me. I'm taking a written test instead."

"That seems pointless." Victoria giggled. "In my old school, we'd get an extra study hall, although I never got any work done."

"Lucky you."

The heavy backpack pressed into Victoria's legs. She let it slip onto the floor, holding it between her knees. One more book and she'd have to buy a new backpack or risk the whole thing exploding in the hallway.

"It wasn't easy walking to the bus stop." Hannah massaged her ankle. "Maybe you can help tomorrow."

"Sure, I'll give you a shoulder to lean on. What time should I come over?"

"No, I meant create something for me to ride on." Hannah winked at her. "It only has to go from my front door to the street corner."

"Don't even talk about it." Victoria gazed around the bus to see if anyone was listening to them, but the kids were focused on their phones, chatting with their fingers instead of their mouths. "Not a peep."

"Fine," said Hannah. "I'll suffer through another torturous hike on my own."

A mischievous grin meant she was kidding, but Victoria preferred she didn't joke around. Hopefully, her ankle felt better, especially since she didn't bring crutches. If not, Victoria would be happy to walk her friend to the stop each morning. She remained close as they exited the bus and escorted Hannah to the lockers.

As the vice principal made his morning rounds, Victoria waited for him to pass before opening her locker door. She barely had room to exchange books for papers in her backpack. No other students were carrying extra clothing around the hallways, but even her jacket couldn't fit in the locker. With the furnace warming the school to a tropical temperature, however, the cold weather would only be a problem during a prolonged fire drill.

A few spots over, Hannah dropped a page of homework from her binder and winced as she reached down. When Victoria bent over to pick it up, another hand beat her to the task. Brandon returned the paper to Hannah.

"What happened to you?" he asked. "You were fine after the party last night."

"I tripped on the way home," said Hannah. "It's nothing."

"If you need help, let me know."

As soon as Brandon stepped away from her, the two boys who hung around Clare and her gang knocked into him.

"Struck out with Victoria, so you're trying the other one?" Lou said, evoking a chuckle from Mike. "Loser."

Brandon waited for them to get halfway down the hallway before heading in the same direction. Victoria had a vision of herself receiving the same treatment from the popular girls. Without Hannah to take her mind off the mean kids, she would have become like Brandon, afraid of who he might offend. At least he had friends at the lunch table. He didn't have to impress anyone else.

Mr. Wallace, the biology teacher, had rearranged the classroom since Friday. Victoria didn't realize the benches moved, but instead of rows, they formed a semicircle facing the front of the room. A fake skeleton hung from a metal frame in the center, while several posters containing hand-drawn images of animal bones adorned the white board. Victoria doubted Mr. Wallace intended to extend the recent holiday, so they were going to be drawing in class. As long as they didn't have to copy the muscular system, she'd be fine. Anatomical figures without skin disgusted her.

Hannah had already taken out her pencils and lined them up on her portion of the lab bench before Victoria sat down. While Hannah started doodling, Victoria rummaged through her backpack for the proper materials. Luckily, she found her notebook before Mr. Wallace gave the assignment. Each student had to draw the skeleton from three different perspectives. Homework would be to choose the best drawing and label the bones. Victoria gave up on locating her pencils, buried somewhere at the bottom of her backpack, and worked on the assignment in ink.

For most of the period, the only noises in class were pencils and Victoria's pen scraping against paper. Mr. Wallace sat up front reading a horror book hidden below his desk. He paused every few minutes to check on the class. Unlike the rest of the students, Victoria only moved around the room when prime spots opened up at the benches, instead of whenever she completed a drawing. She preferred to sit near Hannah when possible, and far from the popular girls otherwise. If a drawing wasn't done, she'd finish it at home from a picture off the internet. Mr. Wallace would never know the difference. He was lost in his book.

Her second rotation brought her beside Brandon, who reached for his water bottle every few minutes. Victoria moved her work over to guard against a spill before returning to her drawing.

For the next few minutes, Brandon kept his head down while scribbling on his paper. When he went for his drink, he knocked the bottle over. Water flowed over Victoria's drawing, soaking the paper and smearing the sketch. It didn't matter that she knew this would happen. She still couldn't avoid the accident.

"Look what you did." She wiped off her notebook, making the artwork less recognizable.

"Sorry, it was an accident." Brandon grabbed some paper towels from the wash area and handed them to her. "I got water on my drawing, too."

Mr. Wallace looked up from his book and returned to his reading. He didn't care about the disaster.

"Just watch what you're doing in the future." Victoria moved her seat over as far as it went. "Some accidents can't be fixed."

"It's only water." Brandon tore out the ruined paper to start again.

By the end of the class, Victoria and Hannah were the only ones left with their notebooks open. Victoria glanced at Hannah's drawing, which included tiny legs on the bottom of the metal frame instead of wheels.

"What are you doing?" She snatched Hannah's notebook.

"The same assignment as everyone else," said Hannah. "Why?"

"Because I warned you about revealing my secret."

Victoria's voice was loud enough to attract Mr. Wallace's attention. He closed his book and looked up at them.

"Is there a problem, ladies?" he asked on his way to their bench.

"No." Victoria covered Hannah's drawing with her arms.

He held out his hand until she gave him the notebook. Mr. Wallace peeked at its contents.

"Is this yours?"

Hannah nodded.

"You have a vivid imagination." He returned the notebook to her. "In the future, please keep your sketches to what you observe. Do you think Linnaeus would have been as successful if he didn't keep accurate records of his surroundings?"

"No, sir," said Hannah.

"And you?" Mr. Wallace turned to Victoria. "Do you think we're in third grade? Hands off other students' work."

"It wasn't her fault," said Hannah. "I offered her a blank page to write on."

Mr. Wallace gazed at the two of them.

"In that case," he said, "no detention this time, but keep your hands on your own possessions."

He placed a finger on Victoria's drawing.

"Nice lines. It almost comes alive on the paper."

Victoria closed her notebook and shoved it into her backpack, crushing work from several other subjects. She was worried about Hannah spilling her secret. These were innocent drawings, but next could be whispers that start a rumor. Why couldn't they just keep it between themselves? Her life was much simpler before.

As soon as the bell rang, she marched to gym class, glad that Hannah wouldn't be attending. At the rate her friend was going, the entire school would know about her special power by the end of the week. Even if Hannah couldn't convince everyone to believe her right away, a curious few would pry into Victoria's life. In either case, it might be better not to leave Hannah alone for the rest of the day. Victoria considered complaining of an upset stomach to get out of gym, but she'd only be sent to the nurse instead of the exam room.

It was badminton day in gym class. Victoria grabbed a racket from the pile on her way to the basketball court, where four nets had been spread out. The gym teacher, Ms. Macken, separated the students into groups as they filtered in, sending Victoria to the far net with Lou, Mike, and three others. The boys played odds and evens to see who'd be stuck with a girl on their team. If she knew she wouldn't get caught, Victoria would have animated their shoes and caused them to fall when they started playing. She scowled at them and chose the near side of the net. Lou and Mike faced off against her, both sneering back. They must have cheated to be on the same team, but Victoria didn't care which side they were on. She'd beat them either way.

"Clare told me you spilled a drink on her." Lou launched the birdie over the net.

"She dropped the ladle all by herself." Victoria knocked the birdie high into the air. "I wasn't even close to her. Ask anyone."

Lou smashed the birdie back at her. She tried to get out of the way, but it smacked into her arm, leaving a red mark.

"One point for us," said Lou, "and it's still my serve. Send it over."

Victoria whacked the birdie under the net, forcing him to retrieve it. He and Clare deserved each other, bullying other kids to make themselves look better. Someone had to teach him a lesson, and with the kids chatting among themselves, this was Victoria's chance. When he reached for the birdie, she raised her palm, ready to embarrass him.

"Sportsmanship counts," said Ms. Macken. "When you lose a point, please hand over the birdie nicely."

She gave Victoria a slight nod, meaning she'd be watching her. Victoria lowered her hand. She couldn't risk using her power if the teacher was spying on her throughout the class. Besides, another student would notice. She never should have considered the option.

"What about this?" She showed Ms. Macken the welt on her arm.

"That'll fade by the end of the day," said Ms. Macken. "Next time, hit the birdie with the racket instead of your arm."

Lou and Mike chuckled until the teacher looked their way. Victoria couldn't let them get away with taunting her, and she couldn't use her power.

The boys kept the birdie away from her for the next few shots, but she eventually took a swing and knocked it out of bounds on Lou's side. She did the same each time she hit the birdie, evoking many comments about how bad she was at the game, but she accepted their teasing for two reasons. First, she forced Lou to jog back and forth from the court to the bleachers, and second, because Ms. Macken finally heard their taunts and scolded the boys for poor sportsmanship.

Victoria smirked at them and scored a few points for her team. By the end of class, they'd split the games, each side winning three times. Just before leaving the court, Lou sent the birdie whizzing past Victoria's ear as an obvious message. She should have used her ability before. He clearly didn't care about reprimands.

During lunch, Brandon remained at his side of the table, ignoring both his friends and Hannah. Victoria deposited her tray at the spot farthest from him. She shouldn't have been angry that he spilled the water, but people had to accept responsibility for accidents they caused. He needed to apologize more than a quick, "Sorry."

Across from Victoria, Hannah was munching on her peanut butter and jelly sandwich.

"How was the gym quiz?" asked Victoria.

"Did you know you're not allowed to jump when receiving the serve?" Hannah finished chewing her sandwich and took a sip of water. "I guess they didn't want anyone playing the game to get too excited. Isn't that the opposite of most sports?"

"I bet we broke a ton of rules today," said Victoria. "Like purposely hitting people with the birdie."

She showed Hannah the red welt on her arm. It had partially faded but still marked her otherwise pale skin.

"Actually, that's allowed," said Hannah. "Who did it?"

"I was playing against Lou and Mike. They accused me of spilling the drink on Clare."

"You should have... you know, done something."

"I did," said Victoria. "I acted inept and made them run after the birdie a hundred times."

"No," said Hannah. "I meant..."

"I know what you meant. Stop talking about it already."

Victoria took her tray and moved over a few seats next to Brandon. If another table were available, she would have moved there.

"Did I ruin your Bio drawing?" asked Brandon.

"It's fine." Victoria focused on her meal. "Sorry I got angry, but the lab notebook is twenty percent of the grade."

"Mr. Wallace would have understood."

"Would he?"

"Maybe not." Brandon chuckled. "He might have expected you to redraw every page in a dry notebook. I'm glad he didn't assign you extra work."

"Me, too."

Hannah packed away her trash. "I'm glad we're all friends again."

When she got up, she handed a folded piece of crumpled paper to Victoria. "I'll redraw my page if it'll make you happy. See you in English class."

"What's that about?" asked Brandon.

"Just an argument we had in Bio," said Victoria, "but it's over now."

She jammed the paper into her backpack and cleared her tray. Hopefully, this was the last time Hannah would mention her secret. Too many hints and someone was bound to learn the truth. Victoria glanced at Brandon on her way out of the cafeteria. He smiled back, possibly guessing more than he let on.

Chapter X

Too Far

A warm bed begged Victoria not to get up. She imagined the past few days as a dream, with no one else knowing her secrets. If she thought hard enough, perhaps her fantasy would come true and things would go back to the way they used to be.

"It's a school day." Her mom's shout from the kitchen shattered her altered world. "Come down and eat breakfast. You don't want it to get cold."

Victoria chucked her pillow at the door and followed it out of bed. Try as she might, she couldn't change reality, but she could ignore it. Let Hannah say something about her special ability. No one would believe such an outrageous tale. With little time left, she threw on whatever clothes lay at her feet, grabbed a couple of waffles from the table, and ran to the bus stop.

Hannah was abnormally quiet on the bus, not even mentioning Victoria's handful of dry waffles. She would have asked for a sip of Hannah's water but was afraid her friend would tell her to animate another student's thermos. It wasn't easy controlling objects after she granted them life. They weren't puppets, although they tried to make her happy.

The wind kicked up on the short walk from the bus into school, making Victoria wish she'd worn a heavier coat. The mild weather of early fall was gone, leaving only cold gray days to look forward to until spring. Victoria stopped at the water fountain on the way to her locker, but Lou and Mike had surrounded it with their friends, not letting anyone through their ranks. They parted briefly when Mr. Moritz strolled by on his morning rounds through the hallways. Victoria would have forced her way in, but Clare and Belle showed up before her, and she feared doing something regrettable if she faced them as a group.

The first bell rang as Victoria approached her locker. A few nearby kids stepped away from her, probably worried they'd have to help clean the floor if she dropped anything. Lucky for them, there wasn't enough time to swap books and struggle to close the locker door before homeroom started. She'd have to make do with whatever supplies were in her backpack already.

"The offer still stands," said Hannah. "I can help you clear out your locker. We'll stay after school. I'm very good at organizing things."

"There's nothing to clean up in there," said Victoria. "I need all of it."

She didn't know what a teacher might want her to look at in the future. What if the midterm was a collection of questions from past homework assignments? She'd be all set, while Hannah and the other students were scrambling through the dump to find the work they'd discarded. She swung her backpack over her shoulder and headed toward homeroom, with Hannah by her side.

Before they'd taken three steps, Brandon scurried past them at a good clip while occasionally glancing over his shoulder. The gang from the water fountain was running after him. When Lou was within arm's length, he spat on Brandon's shirt, catching him on the collar and causing an outburst of laughter from the onlookers. Brandon neither slowed down nor turned around.

At some point, the boys would have to grow up, but today they acted like children. Victoria kept going toward her classroom until Hannah stepped in front of her.

"Do something," said Hannah. "He's your friend."

"He's fine." Victoria's backpack weighed down on her shoulders. "Besides, the second bell will ring any second. They'll all be in class soon."

"That's not the point." Hannah wouldn't let her pass. "A little teasing here or there might be acceptable, but they shouldn't get away with disgusting behavior."

"Even if I wanted to," said Victoria, "I can't stop every bully in the school."

"I didn't ask you to stop them all."

Hannah scoffed as she removed her lunch bag from her backpack and ran after the boys. Along the way, she unwrapped her sandwich and pulled the pieces of bread apart, letting the aluminum foil fall to the ground.

When she reached Lou and Mike, Hannah slapped one slice on each of their backs, the bread holding fast from the peanut butter and jelly glue. Unfortunately, the incident happened a few feet from the vice principal, who didn't appear pleased with her actions. The gang dispersed, abandoning Lou and Mike.

"It's not what it looks like," said Hannah.

"Is this your lunch?" Mr. Moritz gestured at the soiled shirts.

"Yes, but—"

"Then it's exactly what I think." He peeled the sandwich off the boys' clothing. "Go wash up and get to class. I won't give you a detention for missing the bell if you hurry."

The second bell rang as he dumped the bread into the nearest trash can and faced Hannah with a frown.

"You should be above this childish behavior." He handed her a pair of detention slips. "One for each of the shirts. Stay out of trouble or I'll summon your mother for another talk."

Victoria shrank back as his gaze fell onto her.

"Get to class, young lady," he said. "You're lucky I'm out of slips or I'd write you up for tardiness."

As Victoria passed him, he patted her backpack.

"And take care of your locker. I've had complaints from your neighbors."

Victoria sped up to console her friend, who turned away and stormed off to class. Hannah should have known it was a bad idea for Victoria to use her power in the crowded hallway, although it turned out worse to smear lunch on someone's clothing. Hannah would go hungry this afternoon. And for what? Those boys would have been happy wearing dirty shirts every day if it forced other people to get detentions. Victoria skulked into homeroom with all eyes focused on her. Why hadn't she stayed in bed?

The scowl hadn't left Hannah's face by the time Biology started.

"I would have warned you if I saw him there." Victoria settled into her seat. "Sorry about your detention."

"Detentions," said Hannah. "One for each shirt I ruined."

Victoria chuckled. "It was pretty funny. They matched our Halloween costumes."

Hannah turned her chair away and opened her notebook to a blank page. Victoria felt bad enough that her friend had gotten into trouble, but Hannah's disappointment made it much worse. Instead of using her ability against the bullies or stopping Hannah from making a mistake, she stood by and joked about the incident. If their positions had been reversed, she'd expect sympathy from a friend.

"Well, I am sorry." She found a crumpled sheet of paper to write on. "Lou and Mike deserved worse."

Mr. Wallace droned on about observations and the scientific method for the entire period, but as boring as he was, the next few classes were worse. Unable to concentrate on her schoolwork, Victoria wondered what would have happened if she'd used her power on the bullies. Hannah wouldn't have received a detention, but the school might have discovered her secret. They'd keep asking questions and getting more people involved, when Victoria preferred to be left alone. And it wouldn't have stopped with the students. Reporters would have been next, surrounding her house at all hours. Hannah might not yet understand it had to be this way, but eventually she would.

The clock refused to cooperate during art class. Victoria was tempted to animate the dial and turn it ahead five minutes, but doing so wouldn't have caused the bell to ring any sooner. Maybe it was better not having friends if one argument made her feel this terrible. She'd get along fine with no one prying into her personal life, at least until she was old enough to live on her own.

She looked at the time and groaned. There were still two minutes until lunch period. The scent of fried food wafted through the open door, giving her a pang of hunger. A couple of waffles wasn't enough of a breakfast to keep her satisfied the whole morning. Next time, she'd grab a few snack bars, if she could find somewhere to fit them. She stared at her backpack, which seemed ready to explode. It was time for a bigger one, but she couldn't just toss this one out after it had served her so well these past few years.

Only one more minute before satisfying her hunger and repairing her friendship. Hannah couldn't still be mad at her. Detention wouldn't be too bad. Victoria could wait in the library after school, and they'd walk home together when the sentence was over. It would be more fun than a regular day.

When the bell finally rang, Victoria grabbed her backpack and raced down the hall to the cafeteria, not even slowing when she passed teachers staring through their open doors. Getting detention for running in school would only make her life easier. She and Hannah would hang out together while serving their time.

The cafeteria was offering fried chicken and onion rings today, but Victoria skipped the main course. She wanted a meaningful talk with her vegetarian friend without offending her. After selecting a side salad and extra onion rings, Victoria headed to the lunch table, where Hannah was munching on a few lonely carrot sticks.

"You can take some of my lunch." She offered her tray. "It looks edible."

"No, thanks," said Hannah. "This is all I want."

Brandon and his friends kept to themselves at the opposite end of the table, gazing at the front of the room every so often. Although they were worried about something, Victoria ignored them as she took her seat across from Hannah and dug into her salad. The pale lettuce leaves had wilted in the excess dressing, but the rest of the dish was decent.

After their next peek, the boys huddled around their food and stopped talking. Lou and Mike, who normally sat on the other side of the cafeteria, were walking down the aisle toward the table, with Clare and Belle in tow behind them. Of course, there was no vice principal around when the mean kids wanted to cause trouble. Some people were born lucky.

"Too bad about your detention." Lou stopped beside Hannah. "I figured you must be hungry after losing your sandwich, so I got you this. No hard feelings."

He tossed a pair of drumsticks at her. One fell into the bag of vegetables and the other one into her thermos. Behind him, Mike tore into his lunch, chewing with his mouth open.

"This bird had some mighty tasty wings." He didn't bother swallowing his food. "Next I'll go back for its legs."

Hannah pushed her meal to the center of the table as a duet of laughter broke out from Clare and Belle, who waved their drumsticks at Hannah. Victoria couldn't sit by with her friend in distress, but there were so many kids in the cafeteria. What if they saw her? She glanced around the room. Most of the kids were focused on their own lives, and the few staring this way were drawn to the popular kids' antics, giving Victoria a few seconds to act. Even though it was risky, she had to help her friend. She stared at the remaining piece of chicken on Lou's tray and raised her palm, allowing the drumstick to hop onto a new pair of tiny legs and flick his onion rings onto the floor.

"It's alive." Lou shrieked and fell backward.

He dropped the tray and crashed into Mike, sending them both to the ground.

"The chicken... it had legs," he said. "It knocked my food off the tray."

Hannah doubled over in laughter, joined by Victoria after she returned the chicken to normal. One by one, the students gathered around to view the spectacle until the entire room was roaring.

Lou jumped up and sped out of the cafeteria, leaving his tray on the floor to be picked up by Mike, who seemed utterly confused. Victoria was glad Lou's back had been to his friends, blocking them from witnessing the live drumstick. Mike was probably wondering if this was another prank or if Lou had suffered a hallucination. Behind him, Clare and Belle eyed Victoria. Had they seen something? She could always deny it.

"Maybe I will trade for some food." Hannah grabbed the plate of onion rings with a smile.

"Better watch out for that drumstick," she said, louder than normal. "If you don't eat it soon, it might run away."

"Not if I trap it first." Victoria removed the carrots sticks and sealed the bag with the drumstick inside.

"Don't worry, Lou." She held up the bag for the room to see. "I caught the dangerous creature."

Clare and Belle walked back to their table, unwilling to admit they were part of this fiasco. The rest of the kids filtered back to their tables, while Victoria and Hannah finished their lunch. No one seemed to pay attention to them anymore, including Brandon and his friends, who'd gone back to their normal behavior.

"Thanks for sticking up for me," said Hannah.

"We're friends." Victoria's heart was racing. "What else could I have done?"

She'd used her power to embarrass a bully in a room full of people, and not one of them suspected her. Perhaps she could do more to help innocent victims in the school, as long as she didn't draw attention to herself.

Chapter XI

Therapy

Victoria had finished her homework, but there were still chores to complete. Although tomorrow was trash pickup day, the truck usually arrived so early that she had to bring the garbage can to the curb the night before. She made a quick run through the house, collected the remaining trash, and dumped it before rolling the bin to the end of the driveway. Other neighbors had a minimum of two cans in front of their houses, and one couple up the street proudly displayed an array of six large bins, proving they had the most possessions.

As she turned back toward her house, a car stopped at the end of her sidewalk. Trying to determine who was in the car, Victoria stepped closer. There were few people she wanted to see. The passenger window opened, and Hannah's mother leaned over from the driver's seat.

"Victoria?" she called out.

"What's wrong?" Victoria rushed to the car, her heart racing at the thought of her friend in an accident. "Is Hannah okay?"

"She's fine," said Mrs. Walton, "but she's getting into more trouble at school, which worries me. Do you know anything about these latest detentions?"

Hannah had only gotten in trouble because Victoria didn't stop the bullies, but she couldn't admit anything. The more she said, the more Hannah's mother might pry into the situation. Besides, the latest detentions happened after they'd become friends, and Hannah's mother might look for someone to blame for Hannah's recent problems. Maybe she already knew some of the story and was here to force Victoria to stay away from her daughter. No. She probably called the school to find out why Hannah received the detentions, so she stopped here to ask about something else.

Victoria leaned against the car door. "Not really."

"Oh, aren't you two close?"

"We were," said Victoria. "I mean... we are. Hannah's been my only friend since I moved to town. I don't know what school would have been like if we'd never met."

A few cars swerved around the stopped vehicle. Mrs. Walton shouldn't be blocking traffic for the rest of the night. Someone might get hurt.

"I tried to convince Hannah to go back to therapy," said Mrs. Walton, "but she said she didn't need it. I was hoping you'd be willing to go with her."

"Why would I go to therapy?" Victoria backed away. "I'm fine."

Hannah had told her something, even if it wasn't the full truth. How could she?

"Not for you," said Mrs. Walton. "For her. She might change her mind if you came with us. We'll spend the day downtown, eat lunch at an expensive restaurant, and visit a museum or a gallery."

Victoria's muscles relaxed as she let out a big breath. Her secret was still safe. She waved the next car past.

"Sounds like fun."

"Great! How about I pick you up at nine this Saturday? I'll make the appointment for late morning and reserve a table for lunch nearby."

"I'm busy in the morning," said Victoria, "but I could take the bus and meet you at the restaurant. Can the appointment be after lunch?"

"I'll see what I can do. Are you sure your mom will let you take the bus on your own?"

"She won't mind. I already go to the grocery store to pick up food."

"You do?"

A car honked, causing Victoria to jump.

"Just go around," she shouted. "Can't you see we're talking?"

"I'd better not block traffic anymore," said Mrs. Walton. "Make sure you get your parents' approval."

Her car rolled forward.

"Call me if you change your mind and need a ride."

"I will." Victoria waved at her as she headed back to the house.

A day out with Hannah and her mom would be fun. After the appointment, they'd walk around downtown, go to stores, and see street performers.

When Victoria was much younger, her family had vacationed at a popular beach town. They loved watching jugglers, magicians, and singers perform on the boardwalk. Eli could barely walk and soon became tired. She offered to carry him around if they could stay up later. Her parents agreed after a lengthy debate, but she only held her brother for about three minutes before tiring. Without a word, her dad took over the responsibility, and they had the most entertaining night she could remember. She sighed as she closed the front door behind her.

How could it be Saturday already? Victoria dug through a pile of clothing, looking for her favorite pair of jeans. She'd already put on a green blouse and a gray cardigan, but none of her pants matched the outfit. An alarm on her phone beeped, giving her a ten minute warning for the bus. Any later and she wouldn't arrive at the restaurant on time. Hannah and her mother wouldn't mind waiting a few extra minutes, but Victoria preferred to be prompt.

"Argh!" She tossed a box of leggings out the door.

"What's wrong?" Eli tiptoed through the clothing in the hallway.

"I can't find any pants," said Victoria.

Eli flicked a pair of black wool tights at her with his feet. "What about these?"

"I can't wear those without a skirt or dress," said Victoria. "Everyone would laugh at me."

"Ooh, is this another date?"

"It's not a date." Victoria rolled the tights into a ball and flung them across the room. "I'm having lunch with Hannah and her mother."

"You can tell me the truth," said Eli. "I won't let Mom and Dad know you're sneaking around with a boy."

"Stop talking and help me look." Victoria overturned another box of clothes and hurled them into the corner.

"I'm not allowed in your room."

"Well, this time you can come in," said Victoria, "but only this once."

Eli kept his eyes fixed on her as he stepped into the room. He probably thought she wasn't serious about letting him in, but why would she lie? For a lame excuse to have him grounded? He knew she wouldn't do that. Victoria avoided his gaze as she rummaged through another pile on her knees, digging up old shorts and t-shirts.

"Here are pants." Eli tossed a pair of magenta slacks onto her head.

She tore them off and sent them back.

"Do those look like they match?"

"What about these?" he asked.

He dumped the box of clothing on her with a giggle.

“These aren’t even pants.” She threw the items back at him one at a time.

Her second alarm went off, and she still wasn’t dressed. She wouldn’t make the bus unless she charged out of the house half naked.

“I hate you,” she said. “Now I’ll be late.”

She found another box of clothes and emptied it onto Eli, who laughed as he dug himself out. As soon as he was free, he did a belly flop onto the largest pile in the room. Victoria buried him again. She didn’t realize how much she missed his playfulness until now. Hannah and her mom would have to wait for her at the restaurant, but she’d text them from the bus so they wouldn’t worry.

The next time Eli sent clothes flying, Victoria sorted through each piece until she saw the pair of jeans she wanted.

“You found them.” She jammed her legs into the pants. “Thanks for the help.”

“No problem.”

Eli sent a few more items her way, clearing the hall on his way back to his room. Victoria waited to hear his video game pings before rushing to the bus stop.

Victoria didn’t arrive too late to the restaurant, but Hannah and her mother had already ordered their food. Hannah was wearing a long tan skirt with a matching top, which almost appeared to be a dress. Victoria glanced down at her casual jeans. Perhaps she should have put on something more formal.

“I hope you don’t mind,” said Hannah. “We ordered you a salad to start.”

“Anything’s fine,” said Victoria. “Sorry I’m late.”

“Were you busy this morning?” asked Mrs. Walton. “I heard that you go grocery shopping on Saturday. Hannah has never set foot in a supermarket alone. How did your parents convince you to take on so much responsibility?"

"Oh... I..."

"Mom," said Hannah, "stop trying to get me to do more around the house. You said school was my top priority."

"It is. I was just—"

"Trying to force extra chores on me. Fine, but in return you'll have to trust me more."

Her mom winked at her.

"You mean like spending the day alone with Victoria?"

Hannah nodded with a sly smile.

"I'd have to call Victoria's parents first," said her mother.

"They won't mind," said Victoria.

"Are you sure?" asked Mrs. Walton. "My father never would have left me alone in the city when I was your age."

"They let me go where I want," said Victoria. "Call them if you don't believe me, but you know that I go food shopping on my own."

"Then I'll pick you up at four in front of the therapist's office. That'll give you an hour for shopping after the appointment. Are you sure I can't come along?"

Victoria would have yielded, but Hannah gave her mother a side eye. Lunch together would have to be enough. This afternoon was for teens only.

When the waitress brought the salads, Victoria ordered a bowl of fettuccine Alfredo. It wasn't her favorite dish, but she felt uncomfortable ordering meat in front of Hannah. She wondered if Hannah's mother was also vegetarian.

Victoria's parents would never have considered the option. They loved bacon and sausage in the morning. Victoria could still hear the sizzling strips from earlier today calling her downstairs to a hearty meal with the family. Hopefully, Hannah wouldn't try to convert her. She didn't want to disappoint her friend.

Hannah rushed through lunch, not slowing down to savor any of her food. She clearly wanted to start their adventure as soon as possible, but Victoria kept wondering if she'd ever become bored with eating eggs, toast, and bacon? She poked at her pasta, barely finishing a quarter of the plate by the time Hannah and her mom were done eating.

Before they parted ways, Mrs. Walton pulled Victoria aside.

"Thanks for agreeing to this," she said. "Hannah would have caused a fuss, but now she's so excited to spend the day with you, I could make her agree to five more appointments."

"I'm excited, too," said Victoria. "It'll be fun."

"What are you two whispering about?" Hannah inserted herself between them.

Her mom gave her a big hug, holding onto her longer than Hannah appeared to want.

"Mom," she said. "We'll only be apart a few hours, less than a school day."

"I know, but you're growing up so fast."

Hannah's face went bright red as she rolled her eyes at Victoria. She probably thought Victoria found the scene too childish, but Victoria only smiled back.

The therapist's office was on the third floor of a four-story building, one of the tallest in town. Victoria didn't expect it to be crowded on the weekend, but there were several other families in the waiting room. The doctor must have specialized in adolescence, accommodating non-school hours.

Hannah found two seats in the corner. The white walls and sparse furnishings reminded Victoria of a hospital. She sank into a chair and stared at the magazine covers in front of her. In an hour, they'd be out of this sterile place and on their way to the stores. Thankfully, the appointment didn't start late. She would have been upset if they had less time shopping because the doctor had overbooked her patients.

When the door opened and she was called, Hannah turned to Victoria.

"Come in with me," she said.

"But it's private."

"She and I have already gone over everything." Hannah waved for Victoria to join her. "Now you get to suffer with me."

Victoria wouldn't want anyone else in the room if this were her appointment, but she didn't relish being bored in the waiting room. She followed Hannah through the door.

"You must be Victoria," said the doctor as the two girls entered her office.

A pair of padded chairs faced her desk, which held several knickknacks to distract her patients. A tiny figure of a therapist speaking with a young girl monopolized the corner, while several shells lay scattered around the desktop.

"I heard you took the bus on your own this morning," she said. "Were you nervous?"

"There's nothing to be scared about." Victoria picked up a small murex and felt its rough edges. "I've done it before."

"I found that shell in Florida," said the therapist. "It's my favorite."

"There's no reason for Hannah to be here." Victoria placed the shell on the other side of the desk. "What happened in school had nothing to do with her father."

"That's what I told them," said Hannah. "No one believes me."

"I believe you," said the therapist, "but it's good for us to talk."

"About what?" Hannah squeezed the arms of the chair. "You're the one who convinced my mom I needed another session."

"We can talk about anything you want. Remember, everything we discuss is confidential, not a word to your mother unless you give permission."

Hannah glanced at Victoria, who shook her head, worried her friend wanted to talk about her special power. She should know not to trust anyone else, including the therapist.

"Are you jealous Victoria took the bus alone?"

"Why would I be jealous?" asked Hannah. "She's my best friend."

"Sometimes we can be jealous of our friends. It could be something they own or someone they have a relationship with. Perhaps we think their lives are perfect compared to ours."

Hannah shrugged.

"Maybe her parents give her more freedom because she has more responsibility," said the therapist.

"What are the best stores around here?" Victoria squirmed in the chair, fiddling with the figurine.

"If you're not comfortable in here," said the therapist, "you may wait outside or in the next office. I'm sure Hannah wouldn't mind."

Hannah gave Victoria a silent plea to stay.

"I only asked because I don't want to waste time in bad stores," said Victoria. "This is our first trip downtown together."

The therapist reset the figurine to its original position.

"I don't spend much time in the area except for work." She faced Hannah. "Why don't you tell me more about the detentions?"

"I got them because some bullies needed a lesson," said Hannah. "Unfortunately, the vice principal didn't agree with my methods."

"Which were?"

"A peanut butter and jelly sandwich on their shirts."

Victoria stifled a chuckle when the therapist looked her way. The old woman had no sense of humor.

"I know you're more mature than that, Hannah," said the therapist. "Something prompted you to act out. Did those kids hurt you?"

Hannah peeked at Victoria again. Any more questioning from the therapist and she might break.

"Okay, fine," said Victoria. "She was upset about her father. Can we go now?"

She shouldn't have brought him up, but Victoria was worried Hannah might reveal her secret. The therapist was required to keep Hannah's information private, but Victoria wasn't her patient. The same consideration might not extend to her.

"Have you been thinking about him recently?" asked the therapist.

"I guess so." Hannah pulled her feet up onto the chair and turned her back to Victoria. "He helped me become a better person, and now he's gone."

"What would he think about your actions if he were here?"

"What I did was wrong," said Hannah, "but it was only some food. The two shirts will be good as new after the next wash. My father would have thought the whole thing was hilarious."

The therapist sat back in her chair with her arms crossed. Why was she asking Hannah how her father would have reacted? He wasn't around. It didn't matter what he would have said or done. This conversation would only make Hannah miss him more, possibly enough to affect her in school next week. What did the therapist want? For Hannah to fail her classes and get more detentions?

"She misses her father," said Victoria. "You're only making it worse by not letting her get on with her life."

Victoria jumped up from the chair and stormed out of the office. What was the point of therapy? To make people feel worse about their lives? Distractions were a better way to take one's mind off its problems. Instead of endless talking, the therapist should have brought them shopping. Victoria hopped into the corner chair in the waiting room and faced the wall. Why hadn't she stayed home and played with Eli?

Chapter XII

Self-Doubt

Within days, it was too much of a hassle to open her locker unless she absolutely needed something. Instead, Victoria stood with her back against the wall, watching her friend.

"I can't believe you didn't find a single outfit Saturday." Hannah opened her locker door and selected a few books. "We stopped in so many interesting stores. I would have bought a dozen blouses if I had the money."

While they were shopping, Victoria had found several shirts and some great jeans, but after spending so much to impress the popular girls, she had to budget her money. It didn't matter that she'd returned most of the items. She had fun hanging out with Hannah. It would have been more enjoyable, however, if they'd skipped the appointment. Speaking with the therapist only brought back sad memories, but Hannah had seemed to recover.

"I'll buy something next time," said Victoria. "See you in Bio."

"Wait," said Hannah. "I want to invite your family to Thanksgiving dinner. It's just my mom and me, so it would be great if you joined us."

"Thanks, but we're—"

"Going out of town to spend the day with relatives." Hannah closed her locker and spun the dial. "I figured."

Her defeatist tone brought Victoria's mood down another notch. She loved spending the holidays with her family, but they'd been together all the time since the move. A couple of days apart wouldn't be too bad.

"I can stay behind and celebrate with you."

"That would be wonderful. You can stay overnight," Hannah said with a spring to her voice. "My mom wouldn't mind. Do you really think you won't have to go with your family?"

"They've seen me enough these past few months. One extra holiday won't matter either way."

They were about to head to their respective classrooms when the vice principal blocked Victoria, standing with his hands on his hips.

"Is everything okay at home?" he asked.

"Of course." Victoria eyed him suspiciously, worried about what he'd heard. "Why do you ask?"

"Your parents didn't sign up for the conferences. I've rarely seen that before, especially for new students. The few times I encountered similar situations, there were problems at home. If your mom and dad are too busy for the conference dates, we can accommodate their schedules. Teachers love connecting with parents, even if it's for a few minutes. But if something else is going on—"

"I guess they're confident in me," said Victoria. "Is anything wrong with that?"

"Nothing," he said, "but remember, we're here to talk whenever you want. You can speak with your teachers after school, and our counselors are fantastic listeners."

"Why would I need a counselor?" asked Victoria. "Everything's great. How about you pressure those bullies to seek help? They make life miserable for other students, and no one seems to care."

"Bullying is a serious matter. Our school has a zero tolerance policy. If you've seen anything, you should speak with someone in the front office or file an anonymous report."

"Thanks, I will."

"Transitioning to a new school is never easy." He sauntered away. "I'm glad you're doing well."

Brandon had been waiting a few feet down the hallway. As soon as the vice principal disappeared, he approached Victoria and Hannah. His shirt had crisp creases, his jeans were freshly ironed, and his hair was neatly combed.

"I'm still not ready to date anyone," said Victoria. "Go back to your friends."

"No, I just came over to thank you," he said.

"What did I do?"

"Not you, Hannah." He gave her a quick smile. "Wiping your lunch on Lou and Mike's shirts was incredible. It gave me the confidence to stand up to them. Now, they don't bother me anymore. Thanks."

Hannah smirked at Victoria as she accepted the credit. At least one positive result came from her detentions, but Victoria wouldn't have done anything differently, even if her actions had stopped all the bullying in school. She'd gotten lucky when she animated the chicken. No one else could know about her secret. Let them treat Hannah as the hero. She didn't mind... she supported her friend.

"Can I walk you to class?" asked Brandon.

Victoria nodded at Hannah. She deserved special treatment for helping him, especially given all the trouble it had caused her.

"Why not," said Hannah.

Victoria watched them stroll down the hallway side by side. She wasn't jealous of the pair, especially after she'd turned him down. Why shouldn't she be happy for her friend? Their backpacks bounced synchronously against their bodies while they walked.

Most of the kids had left the hallway, leaving Victoria alone by the lockers. A giggle echoed from Hannah in the distance, laughing at a joke Brandon must have told her. Victoria could have been in her place but had chosen against it. She let out a deep breath and marched toward her next class.

Lunch couldn't come soon enough, although the food didn't compare to homemade. There appeared to be fewer choices than usual. If the cafeteria offered anything Hannah could eat, Victoria would have traded lunches with her. But what if Hannah had already traded with her new admirer? Victoria didn't feel like seeing them together at the lunch table. They'd probably start dating soon and would want to sit next to each other while they ate. She groaned as she considered skipping lunch. Eating was overrated.

The rest of the students didn't share her lack of appetite. They rushed through the halls to deposit their books in their lockers before darting to the cafeteria for a spot in line. For what? Soggy salad and limp pizza? As an older boy raced around a corner, he collided with a girl coming the other way, sending her papers flying into the air.

"Sorry," he yelled and continued to wherever was so important.

Victoria picked up a few sheets, handed them to the girl, and chased the inconsiderate boy.

"They're such jerks," Victoria called back.

"Hey, you're the new student, aren't you?" the girl shouted.

"Yeah." Victoria glanced over her shoulder without slowing. "Can't talk now."

She couldn't stop or she'd lose sight of the boy. If she didn't do something, who knew how many more accidents he'd cause in the future. A simple collision today might become a more serious fender bender in a few years. With no one addressing his irresponsibility, he was destined for a life of causing problems and not caring about the consequences.

Victoria followed the boy through the hall, breaking into a brisk run when there was no sign of teachers. It was too dangerous to call to him. She might draw attention to herself. Thankfully, most of the school had already started lunch, allowing her to use her ability when she got close to her target. Just a few feet more and she'd animate his backpack into tripping him. But would that make her as bad as him? Perhaps she should toss his belongings onto the floor to slow him down—the same as he did to the unfortunate girl. She raised her palm, ready to dole out justice, when a voice barked from an open door.

"No running in the hallway, young lady."

Victoria stumbled a few feet as she came to a stop. Mr. Moritz stepped out of the nearest classroom, where he'd been lurking until he could catch someone. She shouldn't have chased the boy and risked exposing her ability, but why hadn't the vice principal seen him running through the corridor? He was only a few steps in front of Victoria. She gazed down the hallway, but the boy was no longer in view. Some people had all the luck. With a sigh, she lowered her head and apologized for running.

"Shouldn't you be at lunch?" Mr. Moritz pointed down the hallway. "The cafeteria is that way."

"I know," said Victoria, "but I was... going to pick up some homework."

Maybe he guessed she was about to do something mischievous, but he didn't know about her power. And since she never caught the boy, he couldn't punish her for an action she didn't commit. As he reached into his jacket pocket, Victoria prepared to receive a detention. Her first ever.

"Carry on." He wrote a line or two in a small black notebook. "At a reasonable pace. And remember, lunch is not a free period."

She spun around on her heels and marched toward the cafeteria. A bite to eat wouldn't be terrible. She was getting a little peckish.

The lunch line snaked halfway down the hall but moved quickly because of the limited options. When she reached the serving area, Victoria selected a bowl of macaroni and cheese, along with a bottle of orange juice. At the back of the room, Brandon and Hannah had nestled up next to each other at the table. Victoria glanced around the cafeteria for another place to sit, but no one had finished eating yet, leaving her with no options. Her eyes connected with Clare at the popular table. A returned scowl convinced her to select her normal spot. She'd never eat lunch with those girls.

By the time she got to the table, Hannah had moved away from Brandon to her normal seat.

"What happened to you?" asked Hannah. "Half the period's over."

"Nothing." Victoria dropped her tray onto the table, scattering a few noodles from her plate. "You didn't have to change seats for me."

"What? This is where I always sit."

"I know. That's what I was saying."

Hannah bit into her sandwich while shaking her head. She probably wanted to sit next to her new boyfriend. Victoria corralled the loose noodles into a pile, imagining each of them moving around the table on their own. The spectacle would instantly shift Brandon's attention to her, something she didn't want. She lined up a few more noodles before shoveling a forkful into her mouth.

"Is anything wrong?" asked Hannah.

"I'm not hungry after all." Victoria dropped her fork.

"So don't eat." Hannah spun to face her. "We can just talk, or you can get a head start on your homework."

"It's in my locker," said Victoria. "It would take the rest of lunch just to fish it out."

Hannah chuckled, her smile bringing a moment of joy to Victoria. They were still best friends. Hannah could have sat next to Brandon for the entire lunch period, but she chose to eat beside Victoria. Why did she envy Hannah's relationship? They'd remain close no matter who entered or left their lives.

"You can go back to your seat over there," said Victoria. "I'll be fine."

"What do you mean? I've been here the whole time."

Victoria winked at her.

"Of course you have." She took two more bites, washed it down with the juice, and stood up. "I need to find my stuff for class. You two have fun."

As she left the room, she peered back at the table. Hannah hadn't moved yet, probably waiting for Victoria to be out of sight before returning to her place by Brandon. At least she was being considerate. Victoria would show her the same sensitivity. She'd try to be happy for them. Besides, she had too much else on her mind to worry about boys.

When she opened her locker, half the contents spilled onto the floor, making it easier to find what she needed. She picked up the books and papers for her afternoon classes, shoved them into her backpack, and jammed everything else back into the locker, which refused to close. A second space for her belongings would have been helpful. Victoria glanced at the nearest locker. Nobody else had used the space all year.

After making sure no one was around, she gestured at the neighboring lock, granting it temporary life.

"Open up," she said.

The lock spun itself, allowing the door to swing open at the slightest touch. As she suspected, the locker was empty. It might belong to another student, but if it hadn't been used in the first three months, it wouldn't be needed for the rest of the year.

"Thanks." She returned the lock to normal. "This should do for a while."

After depositing half her papers in the new locker, she closed the door. Next time, there might be students around, so she couldn't keep using her ability to open the lock. She glanced toward the office. It wouldn't be difficult to retrieve the combination. The office staff stored everything in old-fashioned filing cabinets. She'd animate something innocuous enough to get past the assistants and search the files, perhaps after school during Hannah's next detention.

Chapter XIII

A Time for Thanks

As Victoria strolled down the sidewalk, she inhaled the scent of turkeys roasting, sweet apples baking, and the ever-present combination of cinnamon, allspice, and cloves. Dozens of extra cars had taken up residence on the street, doubling the population of the neighborhood. Families had gathered together for delicious food, nostalgic talks, and a bit of entertainment, but she wasn't with hers. She was visiting a friend's house on her own.

With the memories of summer warmth long gone, Victoria tightened her coat to ward off a chilly wind. It wouldn't be long before the first snow gave her an opportunity to make extra cash by shoveling driveways. Her family had often spent weekend afternoons traveling around the state looking for the best hills, sneaking onto golf courses until they were kicked off by the winter groundskeepers. Perhaps Hannah and her mom would join them on a sledding adventure one Saturday this season. Victoria frowned at a car that zoomed past, probably trying to avoid being late for dinner. Or the two families could just stay in the area. Why bother searching for a perfect sledding spot, when the hills around the school would be sufficient after receiving a few inches of snow?

A pair of pumpkins framed Hannah's doorstep, and a wreath of dried corn husks hung above the knocker. Although modest, the display showed more holiday spirit than Victoria's house, which looked the same as it did every day since she moved in. A single car graced Hannah's driveway, while the curbside in front remained clear of vehicles. There were no other guests for dinner. Victoria rapped on the door and stood back.

As soon as Hannah opened the door, Victoria knew this wouldn't be a traditional Thanksgiving meal. A blast of garlic and tomato hit her in the face. She handed over a pecan pie from the grocery store as she basked in the zesty aroma. It didn't matter what the main meal was—pecan pie could accompany anything.

"Hey," said Hannah. "Did your family leave for the relatives already?"

"Yeah, this morning." Victoria dropped her overnight supplies by the wall. "They'll be back tomorrow before I get home."

"Good." Hannah grabbed Victoria's pack and brought it upstairs. "I was worried your mom would change her mind and force you to go with them."

"No need to worry."

"It's what my mom would have done," Hannah added in a soft voice. "She doesn't want me out of her sight for long. You saw her before therapy—remember?"

"She might not be ready for you to grow up." Victoria followed her to the bedroom. "Can I help with dinner?"

"It's almost done," said Hannah. "Besides, you brought dessert. I guess we can set the table, but my mom wouldn't mind either way. It's only the three of us, so there's not much work."

"How about we clean up after the meal? It's the least I can do."

"Sure." Hannah raised an eyebrow at her. "That's fine."

"What?"

"You don't come across as the most willing to clean anything."

Victoria stood between her backpack and Hannah. "You mean because of my messy locker?"

"And that." Hannah pointed behind her. "How do you find anything you need in that heap of papers?"

"I don't like keeping things disorganized." Victoria crossed her arms. "But it's impossible to know what I might need one day. Why is it so important to let things go?"

"To make room for new things," said Hannah. "Promise me you'll put food scraps into the compost bin tonight, not back in the fridge for another day."

Victoria scowled at her. This was nothing to joke about.

Dinner was served at five, earlier than Victoria's usual mealtime, but not so early that it seemed like a late lunch. The three settings comprised several plates, two glasses, and a slew of silverware. Other than their lunch downtown, Victoria couldn't remember the last time she dined in luxury. Most of her meals were scarfed down in a rush to begin the next activity, with paper towels substituting for napkins. Even breakfasts were eaten with a looming deadline of making the bus. She'd love to join Hannah and her mother more often if they dined like this every day, but she could always suggest some civilized customs during her own meals at home.

"Before we begin," said Hannah's mother, "let's take a moment to reflect on what we're thankful for."

Victoria glanced at Hannah, who only shrugged. Between completing her schoolwork and keeping her secret safe, Victoria didn't have time for much else. She'd been caught up in her busy schedule for so long that she ignored the good in her life, such as befriending Hannah.

"All right—I'll go first," said Mrs. Walton. "I'm thankful to have such a wonderful daughter."

"Mom, not now." Hannah hid her face behind a sip of water.

"And that we're all healthy and live in a free country," said her mom. "So many others don't have a fraction of what we have, and yet we always want more. Today, I'm glad to be together, including you, Victoria."

Victoria blushed. Was she a bad person for not being happy with her life? For being jealous of her friend?

"Thanks for having me," she said, unable to think of anything further.

"Same here." Hannah lifted her fork. "Can we eat now?"

"Nothing else to add?" asked her mom.

Why should there be? Across from her was a glaring omission at the table. The lack of dishes in front of the fourth seat taunted Victoria. It couldn't have been easy for Hannah. No family should be torn apart by tragedy, especially ones so kind and caring.

"I'm thankful for the food we're eating, especially since I'm hungry," said Hannah. "Are you happy?"

Her mother excused herself into the kitchen and came back with plates of endive and grapefruit. Although the salad was delicious, Victoria missed having her mother's hearty bowl of carrot soup to start the holiday meal. From her reaction to the dish, Hannah would have preferred the soup as well. She poked at the bitter greens and only sampled the grapefruit after sprinkling a teaspoon of sugar on top.

"So, who's your family visiting today?" Mrs. Walton piled the dirty dishes together. "Your grandparents?"

Victoria's grandparents had died many years ago, yet she could still hear their encouraging voices and see their smiling faces. As long as she thought about them, they were never gone from her life.

"They passed away when I was younger." Victoria closed her eyes to picture them. "My family is with... my cousins upstate."

"I'm sorry to hear that." Mrs. Walton returned with a plate of lasagna. "About your grandparents, of course, not your cousins."

Victoria's mouth watered at the tangy dish. It wasn't turkey, stuffing, and sweet potatoes, but it would be tasty.

"I never knew my mother's parents." She waited for the others to be served before taking her first bite. "My dad's mother always gave me cinnamon gum from a pack she kept in her purse. She must have worked at the gum factory, because she never ran out."

"At least your parents have family close by. Hannah's grandparents live across the country. With such busy lives, we only visit them once per year. Maybe we'll try for a second trip this summer."

Victoria focused on her meal, noting three different cheeses in the filling. The lasagna was so filling she didn't miss the sausages her mom used to add to their version of the dish.

"Are any of your cousins our age?" asked Hannah. "I'd feel bad if I took you away from them."

"They're out of college already," said Victoria. "My dad's the youngest in his family, and my mom's an only child."

She finished her portion and sopped up the sauce with a chunk of warm bread. If she hadn't been saving room for pie, she would have had seconds. When Mrs. Walton cleared the plates, Hannah turned to Victoria.

"I'm glad you brought dessert," she said in a hushed voice. "My mom baked cookies, but she tried to make them healthy."

"What's wrong with that?" asked Victoria.

"Try one and you'll see." Hannah scrunched her nose and mouth.

The pie must have been heating in the oven, because Victoria detected the nutty aroma before Mrs. Walton entered the room. Round white cookies surrounded the pie on a flowery plate, making it seem like Victoria had spent all morning baking instead of making one trip to the store.

Victoria bit into a cookie while Mrs. Walton served slices of the pie. It wasn't the sweetest dessert she ever had, but a hint of almond flavor and a flaky texture compensated for the lack of sugar. From Hannah's description, Victoria had expected to crunch on a dog biscuit. Instead, the cookie melted in her mouth.

"Not bad." She reached for another. "May I take a few home with me?"

"Take them all," said Mrs. Walton. "I'm sure she's already told you what she thinks of them."

Hannah went in for a second slice of pie, but Victoria stuck with the cookies. Homemade was far more satisfying than store bought.

After dessert, Victoria hopped up from the table before Mrs. Walton could touch the dishes.

"We'll do the rest," she said. "You can relax."

Hannah collected a few plates with a smile at her mother, who still didn't seem convinced about their offer to help. Eventually, she retired upstairs, leaving the girls to clean the kitchen.

"She enjoys taking care of the house," said Hannah. "As a guest, you shouldn't have to do manual labor."

"I don't have to," said Victoria. "I want to."

She grabbed a dish towel.

"I'll wash." She tossed the towel to Hannah and turned on the faucet. "You dry."

With the two of them working together, it wouldn't take more than a few minutes to finish the task. Back home, she never volunteered to wash dishes. Hannah probably thought she was always this helpful, but the opposite was closer to the truth. Victoria scrubbed the lasagna pan until it was spotless and handed it over.

"Should we load the rest of the stuff into the dishwasher?" she asked.

"Why wouldn't we?" Hannah dried the pan and placed it on the counter. "That's what it's there for."

"Most of the time, my mom washes everything by hand and puts it away. She thinks it'll extend the life of the dishwasher, but what's the point? I didn't know if it was the same here."

"No, load it up," said Hannah. "We'll be done sooner."

Victoria rinsed the plates and silverware before sending them to Hannah, who lined them up on the lower rack.

"After dinner, we'd usually play games." Hannah rested against the counter, waiting for the final few utensils.

"Every night?"

"No, on holidays. My dad kept the television off. He'd only let me watch what I wanted after I finished my homework, and never on special occasions."

"Mine always had to watch a game after the meal," said Victoria. "What's so great about watching sports? Wouldn't it be better to play?"

"If you enjoy that kind of thing. What about at your cousin's place?"

"I'm sure the TV's on full blast already. Where's the aluminum foil?"

Hannah grabbed a box from the cabinet and tore off two large pieces, one for Victoria to wrap the leftover pie, and the other for the cookies.

"You don't have to pretend they're good," said Hannah. "I won't tell my mom."

"I really like them. Why do you keep putting down your mom's cooking? So far, everything she's made has been delicious."

"Your taste buds must be off." Hannah placed the remaining glasses in the dishwasher and closed the door. "My dad and I always agreed about her cooking."

"He was kidding with you," said Victoria. "Maybe he thought it was funny to joke about the food when he actually loved the flavor."

Hannah wiped her hands on a paper towel.

"That still doesn't change how I feel," she said.

She headed upstairs but was stopped by her mother coming the other way.

"Victoria, I think someone's in your house," she said. "I saw a silhouette in the window."

"It's just the television or the lights turning on and off," said Victoria. "I put them on a timer."

"It looked like a person. I should call the police... to be safe."

"Don't call them yet." Victoria reached for her coat. "I'll go check."

"You're not going there alone. I'm coming with you."

"Me, too," said Hannah. "Or do you expect me to stay here alone with a burglar prowling the neighborhood?"

"There's no burglar." Victoria marched toward the front door. "It was a curtain blowing around or a broom falling over. I'll be fine."

Hannah and her mother followed Victoria out of the house. There was no way they'd let her investigate on her own, nor would they wait until tomorrow.

Victoria led them past families having their turkey dinners, past houses filled with laughter and clinking dishes. None of the neighbors would have sneaked around the area in the dark, even to prove nothing was going on.

When they reached her house, a single light was on upstairs. Victoria circled the yard with Hannah and her mom one step behind. She checked that all the doors were still locked before returning to the front walk.

"See," she said. "The doors are closed and no windows are busted. No one's in there."

Hannah sniffed the air. "I smell turkey."

"Of course you do," said Victoria. "Yours is the only house where a turkey hasn't been roasting the whole day."

"And yours," said Hannah.

Victoria stared up at the lit window.

"Yeah, and mine." She hurried to the sidewalk. "And any other one where the family traveled for the holiday. Can we go now? I'm getting cold."

"Sorry about the scare," said Mrs. Walton, "but you can never be too safe. Let's go home and play charades."

Hannah groaned at her.

"Or you two can do your teen stuff together. Don't worry about me."

"We won't," said Hannah.

Victoria pulled her aside. "Your mom might have nothing else to do."

"Don't tell me you like charades."

"Not really, but she seems lonely."

Hannah leaned closer and lowered her voice.

"I thought we'd... you know... try a few things with your ability."

Victoria looked over her shoulder at Hannah's mother, a few steps behind, before glaring at Hannah. She should have known better than to bring up the topic.

"In the morning," she said. "It's been a long day."

"Oh, you're no fun." Hannah gave her a quick grin. "Fine, but it has to be a game other than charades."

"How about Fictionary? It's more fun with a large group, but we can make it work."

"Mom, do we still have that big dictionary?" asked Hannah. "We need it for a game."

"It's in the attic." Her mom jogged forward until she was side-by-side with them. "I'll make the popcorn. You find the book. This'll be like old times."

"Yeah, a blast." Hannah sped up.

Victoria didn't understand why she was against including her mom in her activities. They were still a family, even if she was missing her father. Hannah should have appreciated how much her mother wanted to be a part of her life. Victoria kept pace with Hannah's mom, forcing her friend to slow down.

After the game, Victoria couldn't sleep. She lay awake in her sleeping bag and stared at the ceiling. Although a bed in the spare room was free, she didn't want to be alone. Despite the minor argument earlier this evening, Hannah and her mother were happy together, and Victoria enjoyed being a part of their family, if only for one night. She moved up on her pillow and crossed her arms, preparing for a tedious night.

"You can't sleep either?" Hannah asked from her bed.

"I'm not tired," said Victoria.

Hannah dropped a stuffed bear onto her. "What do you think?"

Victoria crawled out of the sleeping bag and concentrated on the bear, bringing it to life. It jumped onto Hannah's comforter and bumbled across the bed. As it approached her, it stretched out its fluffy arms.

"Okay, that's just creepy," said Hannah. "Now I'm gonna have nightmares."

"It only wants a hug."

Hannah shoved her pillow into the bear's arms.

Victoria should have returned the bear to normal, but she animated the pillow. Tiny arms and legs sprouted from its sides and bottom as the pillow returned the bear's embrace. The two creatures squeezed each other, their gentle hug turning into a wrestling match, each of them trying to pin its opponent to the bed.

"Everything okay?" Hannah's mother called out from down the hall.

"We're fine," shouted Hannah. "Just rearranging a few things."

Hannah rooted for her pillow, cheering each time it gained the advantage. Feeling bad for the bear, who only wanted to be held, Victoria took its side. The match went back and forth for several minutes until the bear wrapped its arms and legs around the pillow. Victoria quickly returned the bear to normal, allowing the pillow to escape defeat and pin its stuffed rival.

"You're safe now," said Victoria. "Nothing to worry about."

Hannah grabbed her pillow and gave it a firm squeeze, kicking the bear to the floor. Victoria took the stuffed animal into the sleeping bag with her. Even though it was no longer animated, it needed company. The bear had only tried to be friendly.

Victoria had to be careful when she used her ability. Not everyone would understand the beings she brought to life. Hannah had just proved that a single innocent creature could be viewed as threatening, turning Victoria into a monster.

"That was awesome," said Hannah. "Good night."

Victoria curled up against the bear and closed her eyes. Thankfully, she was able to ease Hannah's fears. Next time might be different.

Chapter XIV

Detention

Victoria didn't want to return to her regular schedule after the long weekend, but the buses deposited her at school anyway. Teachers hiked from the parking lot with their steaming coffee cups, only to pause before heading inside. Despite the chilly weather, they lingered in the courtyard. Victoria understood their hesitation. The day might never begin if she avoided passing through the entrance. Eventually, however, the first bell rang, summoning students and teachers to the building.

"There's Brandon," said Hannah. "Let's go say, 'Hi' while we have time."

"You go." Victoria waved her ahead. "I have to get a few things from my locker. Don't wait for me."

She hurried for the door before Hannah convinced her otherwise, but glanced back when she reached the front steps. Clare and Belle were leading their game toward Hannah. They probably wanted payback for what Hannah did to Lou and Mike, even though it was insignificant. One pass through the wash would clean their shirts, and no one would ever know anything had happened. The popular girls couldn't let anything challenge their status, however, no matter how minor. They wanted revenge, but Victoria wouldn't let them have it. She rushed forward, ready to use her power no matter what the consequences.

The teachers had entered the building and few students remained outside, most of them focused on not being late for homeroom. Victoria raised her palm and concentrated on Clare's expensive shoes, when Brandon inserted himself between Hannah and the oncoming horde of popular girls.

Victoria lowered her arm, nearly as surprised as Clare and Belle. Brandon hadn't exaggerated when he told her he'd become more confident. He stood with his shoulders back and his head up, staring at Clare's gang. The popular girls turned away from their former target and followed the remaining students into the building.

"I can't believe how fast the weekend flew by." Brandon offered Hannah his arm. "I'm ready for another holiday. How about you?"

Hannah smirked at Clare as she strolled away with Brandon. Victoria gave her friend a quick smile, turned around, and squeezed through the crowd at the front door.

With little time left before the second bell, Victoria sped to her locker and spun the dial. The door flew open on its own, pushed by the mound of materials packed inside. Dozens of papers, writing utensils, and granola wrappers scattered across the floor. Needing more space, Victoria peeked around the hall to make sure no one was near before opening the adjoining locker. She'd only shoved about half the items inside when the second bell rang. Within seconds, the vice principal had gravitated to her side.

"I've already warned you, Victoria." He removed a thick pad from his jacket pocket. "This is for the best."

Mr. Moritz was the only person excited to be back at work, ready to make life difficult for the students.

"It wasn't her fault." Hannah shuffled closer, recovered the rest of the items from the floor, and slipped them into her backpack. "She was holding onto my notes. I must have forgotten to take them back when I was organizing my books."

"You get into enough trouble on your own, young lady," said the vice principal. "You shouldn't be looking for more blame. Lucky for you, I'm feeling generous this morning. Go to class right now... both of you... and I'll forget you missed the bell."

He handed Victoria a detention slip.

"This clutter, however, will be dealt with appropriately, and I know just the person to help."

It had better not be another therapist. The one session with Hannah had been enough.

"Ms. Fila did wonders for my office."

He marched down the hall, searching for other students to punish, while Victoria stared at the detention slip in her hand. She'd never received one before. This morning could have gone much better. She held the second locker open for Hannah, but her friend didn't return the papers to their home. Hannah fished them out of her backpack and held them up.

"What are you doing with this junk?" she asked.

"It's not junk," said Victoria. "I might need it."

Hannah separated out a pen with an empty ink cartridge.

"This isn't trash?"

"I was planning to buy more ink." Victoria snatched the pen away and dumped it in the locker. "I just haven't gotten around to it yet."

Hannah sent her hand back into the pile and extracted two granola bar wrappers. The inner foil sparkled under the fluorescent hall light.

"And these?" She crinkled the wrappers. "Were you planning to fill them with snacks and tape them shut?"

She strolled to the nearest trash can and tossed them out. How could she do something like that? They didn't belong to her.

"What if I need them? I might want silver foil for a project in art class."

"Then I'll buy you a pack of granola bars," said Hannah. "I'll even be nice enough to eat the food before giving you the used wrappers. You can't tell me all the stores will run out of granola bars this year. Are you happy now?"

Victoria was far from happy, but she couldn't do anything about it.

"We'd better get to class." Hannah closed both locker doors and spun the dials. "If Mister Serious sees us here, he'll give us detentions until the end of the year."

She scurried down the hallway, while Victoria remained behind to stare at the trash can. If Hannah was right about the wrappers, why did she feel attached to them? Footsteps echoed from a nearby corridor, prompting her to pull herself away from the trash can. If she hadn't already been late for homeroom, she might have fished through the garbage to retrieve her belongings. Instead, she headed for class, wondering if she should thank Hannah or be angry at her.

Friday arrived sooner than Victoria expected. She was looking forward to a relaxing weekend.

"You going to be fine today?" asked Hannah when Victoria joined her on the bus.

"Sure, why?"

"Because of detention."

"Oh, I forgot about that." Victoria swung her backpack off her shoulder onto the floor.

"Really?" said Hannah. "My first detention was awful. My mom was so disappointed in me."

"It's fine. My mom understood."

"That's great," said Hannah. "But until today you had a perfect record. This one mark against you doesn't have–"

"It's not a problem." Victoria folded her arms across her chest and faced forward. "I don't want to talk about it."

Hannah complied with her request and didn't speak about it for the rest of the day. After the last bell, Victoria deposited Hannah in the library and headed for the detention room. Despite their earlier argument, she couldn't wait for their walk home together.

"Welcome, Victoria," the teacher said from behind her desk. A flowing blue ribbon held her hair in a bun, and a thick pair of glasses framed her eyes.

Victoria didn't recognize the young woman, but she'd only met a handful of teachers during the past few months. She glanced around the room. No other students had shown up for detention.

"It's just the two of us." The teacher bent over to grab something from under her desk. "I'm Ms. Fila. You might have me for precalculus in a couple of years."

Victoria squeezed past the first row of seats, eyeing a spot in the back.

"Don't get too relaxed." Ms. Fila held out a plastic bin. "Please empty your locker into here and bring it right back."

"Do I have to?" asked Victoria. "Can't I just do my homework?"

Ms. Fila shook the bin.

"This is the only work you'll be doing this afternoon. You'll be quite pleased when we're done."

Victoria already knew everything Ms. Fila would say to her, but even the best teacher in the school couldn't predict the future. No one could foresee what would happen or what things might be needed some day. She'd wind up carrying everything from her locker to the room and back again, no better off when detention was over. Ms. Fila didn't seem to care. She was stuck here either way.

"This won't be big enough to hold everything from my locker." Victoria yanked the bin away from the teacher.

"Then make two trips," said Ms. Fila, "or three. Whatever you need. Just don't dawdle in the hallway. We have a lot to discuss."

Who was she to impose her will on Victoria's belongings? Was her office spotless and her house devoid of trash? With a groan, Victoria left the room, resigned to wasting the next hour of her life.

Victoria sat in a chair behind a stack of books and school supplies, unable to see the whiteboard in front of the classroom. Her empty backpack lay on the floor next to her feet, while the surrounding desks were covered in piles of papers, wrappers, and miscellaneous school supplies. It had taken the whole period to empty both lockers and sort through the material, with Ms. Fila helping her place each item.

"Do you understand what we've done here?" asked Ms. Fila.

"Violated my personal property?" Victoria sank back into the chair, waiting for the next few minutes to end.

"We've created three piles." Ms. Fila hovered over the books.

Victoria saw five without turning her head.

"These items are used every day." She put her hand on the top book. "They belong in your locker or in your backpack, depending upon when and where they're needed."

She drifted to one side and grabbed an empty water bottle.

"This is trash," she said. "It goes into the garbage cans or recycle bins."

"But I might—"

Ms. Fila pranced to the other side of the room. "You won't need any of it... ever."

She couldn't be sure. Even Victoria didn't know what she might need in the future. Just because something was broken, didn't mean it wouldn't still be useful. Old pens could get refills, papers with one side covered in writing could be used for scribbling notes, and with Victoria's ability, anything could be made into a living creature, if only temporarily.

"And finally, these things go home with you." Ms. Fila pulled out a graded geometry quiz. "Maybe your parents would like to see your grades, or you might use them to study for midterms. You don't need them in school every day. Just think how much extra space you'll have in your locker."

She returned to Victoria's desk and piled the books into the empty bin.

"You may put these back in your locker," she said, "or in your backpack if you need them for homework this weekend. The same goes for your school supplies, although I recommend only keeping a handful of pens and pencils. Worst case, you can borrow from a friend."

Victoria understood what Ms. Fila was saying, but she didn't feel it was necessary. As long as she wasn't bothering anyone else and cleaned up anything that fell, did it matter what she stored in her locker? That was supposed to be her own space. Did the vice principal think no one else in the school dropped anything by accident? He'd go through a detention pad each day if he monitored every little spill. She lugged the bin out the door, planning to argue with Ms. Fila if any possessions went missing during her absence.

Although the books and supplies would have fit in her locker, she placed a couple of items in the adjoining space. She might not need the extra room now, but she'd make use of it by the end of the year. Before closing the door, she stood back for a better view of how organized her locker appeared. Each subject had its own space, allowing her easy access to important books and materials. It wouldn't be terrible to keep it this tidy all the time.

Victoria returned to the detention room, ready to fight for the rest of her belongings, but Hannah had already joined Ms.

Fila. Together, they'd cleared off two desks, filling the waste basket and overflowing the recycle bin.

"I figured the two of you were in on this together," said Victoria. "Why don't you junk my backpack, as well. It's getting a little frayed on the edges."

"Hannah was only helping so we could leave sooner," said Ms. Fila. "There's no conspiracy against you. We want to make your life better."

Victoria crossed her arms. There was nothing anyone could do to improve her life.

"We're almost done." Hannah hovered over the pile scheduled to go home with Victoria. "Do you think we can fit this in your backpack, or should I carry some?"

Victoria threw the empty bin onto the teacher's desk, grabbed her backpack, and shoved papers inside. She didn't need help.

"So… your first detention is finally over," said Hannah. "Did your mom really understand?"

"Well, she wasn't happy," said Victoria, "but she's not the most organized person, so she couldn't say anything about my messy locker."

"My mom freaked out," said Hannah. "She doubled my therapy sessions for two months after it happened. Now she gets upset and tells me I should talk to her more often."

"You should." Victoria stuffed a few more papers into her backpack. "While you still can."

"What's that supposed to mean?"

Victoria slung the backpack over her shoulder.

"It means we'll be in college soon," she said, "and then in the workforce. You know how busy people get, always forgetting to keep in touch. There's a thousand songs and movies about it."

"I'd never be like that," said Hannah. "My mom and I are close."

Ms. Fila stopped Victoria on her way out of the room.

"Please keep your belongings organized from now on," she said. "A few seconds to straighten up here and there is much better than spending an afternoon in detention. Don't you think?"

"Sure, thanks," said Victoria.

If she needed a single item that had been discarded, she wouldn't spend her money to replace it. Someone else would pay, and she knew how to make it happen. Hannah followed her into the hall with a self-satisfied smile.

Victoria glanced back at the full recycle bin.

"Don't worry about those things," said Hannah. "You won't miss them."

Victoria wasn't sure Hannah was right, but the more she distanced herself from the room, the further she distanced herself from her former belongings. What was there to worry about? If she needed anything that had been thrown away, Hannah promised to help. Perhaps it was acceptable to say goodbye to those items.

By the time Victoria and Hannah were in the main corridor heading for the front door, the recycle bin was a fading memory. She couldn't have done it without her friend's support.

"You've been quiet since detention ended," said Hannah. "Don't tell me you're still upset we threw away a few pieces of trash."

"I was thinking how much lighter my backpack will be on Monday," said Victoria.

"And what about your locker?"

"What about it?"

"You won't need that extra space anymore," said Hannah, "or didn't you think I noticed? I'm glad Mr. Moritz didn't know the other locker was supposed to be empty. If he thought you'd claimed the space, he would have given you a weekly lecture with Ms. Fila."

"Good point." Victoria turned around. "I left stuff in there, but since I don't need the space, I'll clear it out before someone gets suspicious."

"I thought you emptied it at the beginning of detention."

Victoria led her to the row of lockers.

"I wasn't ready to change my ways yet." She opened both doors and moved everything into her own locker. "But now I'll try."

She spun the dials on both lockers in unison, feeling as if she'd just dropped all her books after carrying them for a year. Her life was finally improving. It wouldn't even have upset her if Brandon and Hannah were going out later. She eyed her friend. Hannah seemed bouncier than usual. Perhaps she and Brandon had a date scheduled.

Chapter XV

Cleaning House

The late bus had already left, but Victoria wanted to walk home, anyway. Bright sunlight had broken through a thick layer of clouds and spread enough warmth to leave her jacket hanging out of her open backpack. Nearby, Hannah seemed content to stroll along without speaking. Perhaps she thought Victoria was still upset about detention, but what if she was keeping a secret about Brandon?

"Do you have plans this weekend?" asked Victoria.

"Are you asking me to continue the work from detention?" Hannah avoided her gaze. "It's satisfying to be organized. I can come over and help clean your room now."

"I was talking about you and Brandon." Victoria scooted ahead and came to a stop, forcing Hannah to look at her.

"What about us?" The red in Hannah's cheeks belied the truth.

"You've gotten close to him recently."

"You said you only wanted to be friends." Hannah turned her head. "If you've changed your mind, I'll tell him to stay away."

"Don't do that," said Victoria. "I'm happy for you, but he seemed relieved when I told him I didn't want to date. He said he wasn't ready either."

"He might have changed his mind," said Hannah, "or maybe he was embarrassed you rejected him."

"I didn't reject him. It was the truth. I'm not ready to date anyone. You can do what you want."

She continued down the road a few steps ahead of Hannah, wondering why she didn't feel happy for the two of them. It would be terrible to lose her only friend over a boy.

"I'm glad you're okay with us." Hannah skipped forward to keep up with her. "He asked me out on our first date tonight."

"First date? I figured you'd already gone out a few times."

"Of course not," said Hannah. "I would have told you about something so important."

If she were lying to protect Victoria's feelings, it would have made the situation worse. They were supposed to be friends, yet they couldn't be honest with each other. Perhaps that was the problem. It was difficult to remain close to regular friends when a boyfriend took up all of your time.

"Uh-huh," Victoria mumbled as she sped up.

Hannah rushed forward and put a hand on her shoulder.

"If you're upset, I'll cancel the date," she said. "He asked you out first."

Victoria shrugged her friend off and kept going. Since Hannah was willing to stand Brandon up, it proved this wasn't their first date. After getting busted, Hannah stayed behind a few steps, while Victoria turned onto their home street. She needed time alone after such an arduous week.

"There." Hannah caught up to Victoria. "I postponed the date to next weekend."

That wasn't any different from going out tonight. She needed to be honest with her best friend.

"I'm sorry for making you feel abandoned," said Hannah. "You needed someone to talk to after your first detention."

Victoria kept moving. How could Hannah have known what she needed? They'd only met a few months ago and had rarely spoken about each other's history. Hannah didn't know about her past. Victoria could have been on the field hockey team in middle school, or she could have taken piano lessons. Anything was possible.

"How about we organize your room until dinner time?" asked Hannah. "Or we can just sit and talk."

"No, thanks," said Victoria.

"You never invite me over," said Hannah. "What are you hiding there?"

"I'm not hiding anything. Fine, come over so you can throw away more of my things. What do you care? They have no meaning to you."

"I thought you weren't mad about the garbage I tossed." Hannah walked backward in front of her. "What's really going on?"

"Nothing."

Victoria gazed at her house in the distance as she removed her backpack from her shoulder. This was her chance to reconnect with her friend. It didn't matter how close Hannah and Brandon had become. This afternoon would be for the two of them.

"Sorry I got angry before," she said. "You can come over and help me find room for these things, but we're not throwing anything away."

"You're not making it easy for me." A big smile lit Hannah's face. "But I'm sure we can work something out."

"One would hope."

Side by side, the girls cut across the empty driveway to the front steps. Victoria unlocked the door and dumped her backpack near the living room entrance. Hannah followed her in and hopped onto the sofa.

"Where is everybody?" she asked.

"Eli must be at a friend's house," said Victoria, "and my parents are probably at the supermarket. There should be a note around here."

"I thought you did the food shopping." Hannah placed her backpack on the coffee table. "At least that's what my mom told me. Was it only a ruse to get me to do more chores? You wouldn't try to trick me, would you?"

Victoria's heart raced as a wave of panic hit her. She took a deep breath and backed out of the living room.

"I go to the supermarket when my mom asks me," she said. "Weekends are best because there's no school, but if they went out, we must be low on supplies."

"Speaking of food," said Hannah, "I'm hungry. What kind of snacks do you have?"

"Kitchen's at the end of the hall." Victoria headed for the stairs. "I'll meet you there in a couple of minutes."

"I'm not rifling through your cabinets for a snack. Didn't your mother teach you how to entertain a guest?"

"I suppose not." Victoria glanced upstairs. "Okay, let's find something to eat."

She led Hannah into the dark kitchen. The shades were drawn on the far wall, allowing specks of light to dot the area. Victoria flicked the switch, displaying a barren room. No pots or pans were in sight, and an empty table stood in the middle of the dining area. She opened the refrigerator, revealing an open carton of orange juice, a few apples in the fruit bin, and a row of nearly empty jars lining the door.

"I see why your parents went shopping," said Hannah. "It couldn't wait until tomorrow unless you were planning to eat out tonight."

"I guess they've been eating more for lunch than I realized," said Victoria. "I'm sure they left something for us to nibble on."

She swung the refrigerator door shut and tried a cabinet, uncovering an old box of crackers.

"How about peanut butter and jelly on these?" She took down the box.

"I don't think we have a choice."

While Hannah collected the jars from the refrigerator, Victoria retrieved a single plate and two knives from the cupboard. They assembled the snacks together. Victoria slathered a layer of peanut butter on the crackers and Hannah added the jelly.

"Thanks for postponing your date," said Victoria. "I didn't realize how much detention bothered me."

"I'm glad you're feeling better now." Hannah slapped the two halves together and arranged the finished crackers in a circle on the plate.

They returned to the living room with the snacks, along with two glasses of orange juice. Hannah gazed around the room while she munched on a mini-sandwich.

"I can't believe your mother keeps this place so neat and doesn't force you to clean your room."

"Sure, she wants me to straighten it up, but once I became a teenager, she told me it was my responsibility. If I let her, she'd clean it out tomorrow, even more heavy-handed than Ms. Fila."

"I'd lose my allowance if my room were messy for more than a day," said Hannah. "Maybe you can have your mom talk to mine."

"Why? Don't you like having a clean room?"

"It's fine." Hannah stopped chewing and stared at Victoria. "But I was kidding. My mom would never listen... except to the therapist."

"Oh, sorry." Victoria left the final two crackers for Hannah and headed for the staircase. "I'll be right back. I just need to —"

"What's with you and those stairs?" Hannah jumped off the sofa and rushed past Victoria to the base of the staircase. "Look at that mess up there–boxes everywhere. Did you really think you could stop me from seeing it? We were going up to your room after the snack."

"I was supposed to clean this when I got home." Victoria followed her upstairs. "You only promised to help with my room. I wanted to hide the rest of it somewhere."

"It's lucky I came with you," said Hannah. "We'll make quick work of this disaster, in your room and out here. What is this stuff, anyway?"

"We haven't finished unpacking." Victoria approached several cardboard boxes in the hall. "We don't have to worry about most of these. My parents will take care of their stuff another day. We just have to deal with mine."

"No wonder your house looks empty." Hannah craned her neck for a better view of the boxes before retreating into the bedroom. "Half your stuff is packed away."

"This proves how little of our things we need."

"I'm glad we never had to move," said Hannah. "What a hassle."

Victoria closed the door after shoving aside some dirty laundry. Her room didn't seem too bad, other than the bed not being made and a few items of clothing scattered about. No teenager had the time to keep everything spotless, between spending hours at school, completing homework, and having a social life.

"It looks like a hurricane swept through here," said Hannah. "How do you get any work done?"

"I manage. Should I create a few helpers?"

"As much as I'd like to see this mess clean itself," said Hannah, "having things move around won't do anything. The bigger job is to determine what stays and what goes."

"I told you we're not throwing anything away."

"Even you don't believe that." Hannah cleared a stack of papers off the dresser, adding them to a pile of school supplies in the corner. "Can we use the hallway for temporary storage?"

"Go for it."

"After we free up some space in here," said Hannah, "we can move things back to their proper locations or get rid of them. You've collected so much junk in the past few months, or did you choose to unpack this stuff first?"

"None of it's junk!" Victoria hovered near the door. "As long as I can find what I need, everything has its place."

"Really? I thought you got over your hoarding tendencies this afternoon."

"I'm not hoarding anything."

Hannah pushed through the clutter, stopping in each corner of the room to sift through piles of clothes, books, and papers. She fished a gold chain out from a few socks and placed it with the rest of the jewelry on the dresser.

"I don't see any difference between this room and every house on those hoarding shows… except you don't have a rat infestation."

"If this is so bad, show me one piece of garbage." Victoria leaned against the door. "I dare you."

Hannah bent down where she stood and picked up a blue cardigan.

"That's the sweater my parents gave me when I started middle school." Victoria held out her hand for Hannah to return it. "How could you even think I'd get rid of it?"

"The fabric's pilled." Hannah stuck her hand through the armpit of the sweater. "And there's a hole in the sleeve. If you didn't have four other sweaters in sight, I would have recommended repairing this one, but it can go."

Victoria snatched it away from her, rolled it into a ball, and tossed it onto the nearest stack of clothes.

"I'll sew it when I have a chance," she said. "I told you there's no garbage in my room."

"Fine, what about this?"

She reached for an empty shoe box, but Victoria lunged forward before she could touch it.

"I'm going to keep pencils and pens in there." Victoria clutched the box close to her chest. "You should know how important it is to be organized, but I haven't had the time. It's difficult adjusting to a new life."

"The move has been hard for you," said Hannah, "but I'm here to help."

She collected some school supplies and held them out until Victoria offered her the shoe box.

"If we don't finish this afternoon, I'll come back this weekend." She dumped everything except a broken pencil into the box. "Don't tell me you need this."

"As soon as I find my pencil sharpener, it'll be good as new."

Hannah grabbed a handful of pencils from the box, all of which were full length and had pristine erasers on the ends. Some of them hadn't been sharpened yet.

"This should be enough pencils until you graduate college," she said. "You don't need to keep one tiny nub with a wire rim where the eraser used to be."

"But Eli used it to draw a picture of me."

Victoria held out her hand, but Hannah didn't return the pencil. She only stared back with a look of exasperation. Didn't she care about sentimental items?

"Do you want me to help or not?" asked Hannah. "I have better things to do than argue about what is or isn't garbage."

"Then go do them." Victoria yanked the pencil away. "Go enjoy your date with Brandon if it's more important."

"I think I will." Hannah nudged Victoria aside and opened the door. "You're on your own until you listen to reason."

"Good."

Victoria followed her downstairs and slammed the front door after she left. Why couldn't anyone understand how important certain possessions were to her? You wouldn't throw out an heirloom because it tarnished with age or had a layer of dust on it. Hannah must have mementos from her father that Victoria would consider trash, but she'd never force her friend to throw them away.

She ran back up to her room, tossed everything off the bed, and let the tears flow.

Victoria spent most of the weekend in her room. When she wasn't studying or writing chapter notes, she was listening to a playlist of sad music on her phone. Her only breaks came at mealtimes, when she dined with her family. After a series of nightmares on Friday, she stayed awake most of Saturday night to avoid the bad dreams, but by Sunday evening she couldn't avoid drifting off to sleep.

She was racing home in the dark, desperately trying to reach safety before she was caught. Each hill sapped her energy, forcing her legs to move slower against her will. It felt like she was running through water, although no raindrops graced the dry road. She looked over her shoulder. Nothing. They were back there somewhere, chasing her, but she'd have enough time to reach her house and escape whatever torture they'd planned. Her old home loomed on the hill ahead of her, with lights on both upstairs and down. She took a deep breath and dashed the remaining distance as fast as she could.

When she made it to her house, she opened the door to find it dark inside, despite all the lights being on. A sense of dread swept over her body, freezing her in place.

"Mom? Dad?" she called out. "Eli? Is anybody home?"

No one answered her plea, not even an echo of her voice against the barren walls. They'd moved away without telling her, leaving behind an empty shell. Victoria had to find her family, no matter where they'd gone. She peeled herself from the doorway and fell backward into the road, where a car's tires screeched as its headlights shined in her face.

Victoria jumped awake to her alarm beeping and the Monday morning sun shining through the shades. She threw her pillow at the window. The world should have allowed her extra rest, yet it refused to yield to her wishes. She kicked the covers off but remained in bed until the snooze alarm startled her. Time to start the week.

Sitting alone on the bus, Victoria stared at Hannah a few seats ahead. She'd wanted to sit next to her friend, but Hannah might have rejected her. When they reached school, Hannah merged with the swarm of kids filing into school, forcing Victoria to take up the rear. She couldn't go on like this.

As she approached her locker, Victoria considered how to apologize to Hannah, but a sneer from her friend destroyed her hopes of reconciliation. Perhaps she should return home and go back to sleep. Being alone would make school too difficult for today. No, she wouldn't give up on their friendship, even if it took the rest of the week to win Hannah back.

After the first bell rang, she marched up to her friend, confident about her plan. "I'm sorry about the way I acted on Friday. Please forgive me."

"I don't understand." Hannah eyed Victoria's backpack. "Were you lying to Ms. Fila and me about letting go of those old wrappers and bottles? You said you were fine with it, but you could have told me the truth. We're supposed to be friends."

"We are friends, and I wasn't lying." Victoria grabbed a handful of papers from her backpack and tossed them into the recycle bin. "It was… too much at once. I needed more time."

"I can give you time to adjust." Hannah retrieved the papers. "But you might need these quizzes. Midterms are only a few weeks away."

"Don't remind me," said Victoria. "Are we good then?"

Hannah gave her a broad smile, erasing any thoughts of loneliness. Unfortunately, Victoria still felt they weren't being completely honest with each other.

Chapter XVI

A Friendly Game of Volleyball

The worst part of school was changing clothes in the locker room before gym. Victoria didn't enjoy changing after class either, but at least the period was over by then. Now she was dreading what was next. Volleyball. Thirty-eight minutes of athletic kids pounding balls into the bodies of the less physically gifted.

Being taller than most girls helped, and Victoria wasn't uncoordinated, but even when she bumped the ball properly, it left a throbbing welt on her arms. She was surprised such a painful sport was allowed in school, although if football wasn't banned, neither would volleyball.

She opened her gym locker, stuffed with old clothes and sneakers. When she had some space in her backpack, she'd take it home to wash, but as long as she found something semi-decent to wear, that day could be postponed. Victoria selected a pair of shorts and a tee shirt she'd only used twice and quickly swapped clothes behind her locker door.

Clare and the popular gang were chatting about nothing as they took their time changing. None of them cared how little they were wearing. Prancing around the locker room, they could have been in their bedroom at a slumber party. As Belle passed by, Victoria lowered her eyes, knowing they'd pounce on her at the slightest provocation. It was too draining to stand up to them before a full period of sports.

"Don't hide back there," said Belle.

Victoria's heart skipped a beat. She jammed her school clothes into the locker without looking up, hoping Belle was talking to someone else. After her difficulties with Hannah, she didn't need more problems today.

"Leave her alone," Hannah said from across the room.

Why couldn't they have had lockers close together like in the hallway? So much for staying out of the conflict. Victoria peeked around her locker door, preparing to defend Hannah from the others.

Belle had approached Mina, the shortest girl in gym class, but Hannah had distracted her. Clare faced Hannah, while the gang hovered nearby.

"Your boyfriend isn't here to protect you." Clare leaned closer than necessary. "Now, what did you say to Belle?"

"I said, 'Leave her alone.'" Hannah stood her ground, defiant against the entire group of popular girls.

She shouldn't have drawn attention to herself, especially with the vice principal looking for any excuse to give out detentions. Thankfully, he couldn't enter the girls' locker room. A few rows away, Mina frantically changed her clothes, hiding behind her locker.

"We both know you won't do anything," said Hannah. "Detention would cut into your shopping schedule. Me? If I get another detention, I'll just get an early start on homework. Shall we make enough noise to convince Ms. Macken to investigate?"

Victoria chuckled and slammed her locker, garnering everyone's attention.

"I'm ready for extra noise." She banged on the locker door. "Detention wasn't so bad."

Clare threw her head up and pranced away, leading her group into the gym. On the way out, Belle knocked Mina's locker door shut.

"It took you long enough to join in," said Hannah.

"You weren't doing too bad on your own."

Victoria had never spoken to Mina, but it felt good to defend someone else. Hannah was right about helping others. A simple action had defused a potentially awful situation, and she did it without using her power.

"Thanks." Mina opened her locker to put her street clothes away. "Those girls can be so mean."

"They're just testing who will stand up to them," said Hannah. "They don't like confrontations. By the time Victoria and I are done with them, they'll be model students. Right?"

"Uh... yeah," said Victoria. "We'd better get out there. Class started already."

She shuffled into the gym, where Ms. Macken was separating the kids into teams. Two large nets divided the room into a pair of volleyball courts. Victoria expected half the kids to be sent to the bleachers to wait their turn, but the teacher kept pointing to one side of each court or the other until everyone was on the floor. Of course, Hannah had been sent to the opposite side from Victoria, promising to make gym class even worse. At least they were playing on the same court.

"Sneak under the net." Hannah gestured to her. "While she's not looking."

Victoria glanced at the teacher, who was bent over a bin searching for the perfect ball.

"Quick," said Hannah, "you don't have much time."

As much as Victoria wanted to be on Hannah's team, she couldn't disobey the teacher. Besides, if Hannah wanted to be on the same side, she could have moved just as easily. Victoria shrugged at her and found a spot near the back. A shrill whistle pierced the air, signaling the start of the game. Ms. Macken rolled the ball under the net to Hannah's side.

A girl from the volleyball team took the ball behind the baseline and launched a serve, which sailed over the net toward a cluster of Clare's friends. They ducked out of the way to avoid any chance of colliding with the ball. Ms. Macken held her arm out to Hannah's side and gave a quick toot on the whistle.

"Don't be scared." She put her fists together and squatted down. "Hold your arms out like this and let your legs do the work."

Victoria doubted Clare or her gang cared about improving their volleyball game, especially if it might mar the perfect skin on their arms. A few paces backward allowed her to survey the court—ten kids on each side. This wasn't so much volleyball as dueling games of dodgeball.

The next serve came straight at Victoria. As she maneuvered into a better position, a cacophony of shouts from both sides of the net distracted her. Half the kids yelled at her to miss, a few called the ball out, and some just enjoyed making noise. The bottom of her shoe caught against the polished floor, and she fell, allowing the ball to soar over her head.

"Out," the girls near the back line yelled, drawing a whistle of agreement from Ms. Macken.

A hand from one of the sporty girls helped Victoria up, while laughter echoed in the background. Ms. Macken ignored the taunting and rolled the ball to Mina, eliciting a round of jeers from the popular girls. The teasing upset Victoria more than the laughs at her stumble, but she dared not do anything that would get her caught. Perhaps there was a simpler solution.

"Ignore them." She patted Mina on the arm. "You got this."

Mina tossed the ball up and smacked it with her palm. The ball arced over her teammates but came up short of the net, rolling off to the side. It would have been easier to quiet the popular girls if the ball had gone over, but life was never easy. While Ms. Macken chased the ball, Clare maneuvered across from Mina on the other side of the net.

"Nice job," she said. "Next time you might even reach the net."

Her gang chuckled at the jab.

"Like you can do any better," said Victoria. "The lot of you are afraid to touch the ball."

As soon as she'd finished speaking, she knew she was in trouble. Ms. Macken headed toward her with a frown. The popular girls always knew when to keep quiet and when to tear into someone.

"Sportsmanship is part of your grade." Ms. Macken eyed Victoria. "Try to be supportive of your teammates and your opponents."

Victoria wasn't surprised she'd gotten scolded. The worst of any situation always found her. If she wanted justice, she'd have to take it for herself.

Clare brought the ball to the back of the court, held it up in Victoria's direction just to prove her wrong, and served. The ball headed for the net. Victoria would have been overjoyed if it fell short, but the ball inched over, landing squarely between two popular girls. Ms. Macken didn't care that the girls avoided the serve. She even complimented Clare on her ace. Victoria scoffed to herself as she squeezed her fingers into a fist and fought the urge to use her ability. It wasn't difficult to excel at a sport when your opponents were helping you.

A few points went back and forth, mostly between the athletic kids, until the next rotation brought Mina next to Victoria.

"They're bothering me because Mike asked me out." Mina scooted closer to Victoria. "Shouldn't they be angry with him? It's not my fault."

"They'll use any excuse to be mean," said Victoria. "It's who they are."

"I should tell him no, so I can avoid contact with Clare and Belle. I don't want trouble."

"You should do what you want, but I'd forget him." Victoria kept her eyes on the server. She wasn't going to miss this time. "As far as we know, he's playing a trick on you."

"Do you think he'd do that?"

"He might." Victoria ducked as the ball flew over her head and landed out. "If you want those girls to leave you alone, confront them directly. They prefer when kids cower before them."

"I can't do that."

"Then I'll do it for you."

Determined to help, Victoria moved closer to Belle at each rotation, eventually landing next to her on the court.

"Leave Mina alone." She glared at the popular girl. "She did nothing to you. If you're upset at Mike, take it out on him."

"Or what?" asked Belle.

"There is no 'or.' Just leave her alone."

"What's it to you?" Belle faced her, ignoring the game. "Are you adding her to your group of losers?"

Victoria was ready to animate Belle's shirt, embarrassing her in front of the class, but there were too many potential witnesses around. She glanced across the net at Hannah, who nodded back at her, giving approval for whatever she did.

"It's our serve." An athletic girl handed the ball to Belle.

"No, it's Victoria's turn." Belle slammed the ball into Victoria's stomach, causing her to lose her breath.

Victoria grabbed the ball and staggered to the back of the court, trying not to give Belle the satisfaction of a reaction. Focusing on her anger, she pretended the ball was Belle's head and smacked it clear over the net. Hannah dug the return, Clare set the ball, and an athletic girl spiked it down.

"Game," said Ms. Macken. "Half of you switch sides."

Hannah immediately ducked under the net without checking who else was switching sides and made her way to Victoria.

"I thought you had to win by two in this game," said Hannah.

Victoria smiled. "That's only when you have fewer than twenty people on court."

After a giggle, Hannah gestured at Belle, who made sure she was on Clare's team.

"What was that about?"

"They're bullying Mina because Mike asked her out," said Victoria. "Now she's alone with them on the other side."

Because of her position in the rotation, Mina had crossed sides along with a few others. Victoria felt bad that the poor girl was stuck with Clare and her gang for this game. She should have crossed over to protect her, but she didn't want to leave Hannah now that they were on the same side.

Hannah must have felt the same way, nestling closer.

"It looked like you were about to—"

"It's too crowded here," said Victoria.

"Well, they deserve it," said Hannah, "and I can draw their attention."

"Not now."

The first serve headed for Mina, who displayed skill with a good dig. A second and third hit sent the ball back over the net. When all eyes were in the air, a thump resounded from the other side. On the ground, Mina was holding her leg and screaming. Clare and Belle stood beside her, doing their best to look innocent, but they probably knocked her over. Ms.

Macken helped Mina limp off the court, telling the others to keep playing.

"That was no accident," said Hannah.

Victoria glared at the popular girls. "I know."

When the ball came her way, Victoria picked it up, hid behind Hannah, and concentrated on the white sphere. Tiny legs sprouted from the bottom of the ball. Victoria gave the new creature instructions and rolled it under the net toward the popular girls. As Clare bent over, the ball sprang into the air and smacked her nose.

"Ow!" She fell backward, holding her face.

Blood streamed out from between her fingers as her friends crowded around her, drawing everyone's attention.

Victoria and Hannah ignored the confusion and ducked under the net. With Hannah standing between the kids and the ball, Victoria returned the creature to its natural state. She looked around, receiving an approving grin from Hannah. Her secret was still safe.

While Belle helped Clare to her feet, Victoria inched to the front of the onlookers. "Are you okay?"

"Stay away from me, you freak." Clare held her nose, but the blood seeped through.

She and Belle followed Mina's path out of the gym. Two students sent to the nurse in one period.

"We better keep playing." Victoria grabbed the ball. "The game's not over yet."

After rolling the ball to the server, Victoria eyed the spot of blood on the floor. Maybe she'd overreacted. She didn't intend to harm anyone.

Throughout the rest of the day, Victoria saw Clare's fingers bathed in red whenever she closed her eyes. The popular girls were always mean to other kids, but she'd never seen them cause physical damage. They didn't deserve to be hurt, only taught a lesson. She wasn't even sure if Mina had fallen by accident. Victoria didn't know why she'd gained her special ability, but it wasn't meant to harm others.

"Do you think Clare will be fine?" she asked Hannah on the bus home. "She never came back to class."

"Now you care about her health?" Hannah asked. "After what she and Belle did to Mina?"

"But what if I broke her nose?"

"Maybe that was a little much, but at worst, she'll have a sore nose for a few days. Don't worry about her."

Victoria hoped she'd be fine. She didn't want to cause any suffering. A little embarrassment would have been acceptable. Even worse, she couldn't apologize or everyone would learn her secret.

"If it makes you feel better," said Hannah, "we can call her house to see what happened. Her number's in the school directory."

"That would be too suspicious," said Victoria. "But you're probably right. She'll be in school tomorrow, picking on anyone not in her clique."

"We can do something about that," said Hannah.

"Without hurting anyone?"

"No injuries—I promise." Hannah held out her hand to shake. "It'll only take creative thinking and a superpower. You supply the power."

"Deal," said Victoria.

It was time to make the school a more welcoming environment for all students, not just the popular or athletic ones.

Chapter XVII

Playing Superhero

When the final bell rang, Victoria exited Spanish class to find Hannah waiting in the hall. Hannah grabbed Victoria's backpack, groaned at the weight, and headed toward the back of the school.

"Where are you going?" Victoria asked. "The entrance is the other way."

"Today might be the last warm day of the year," said Hannah, "and we need someplace private to talk."

Victoria followed her to the athletic field, empty as Hannah must have known. The teams had either traveled to away games or had taken the day off, leaving the track to the two of them.

"I told my mom we'd be late," said Hannah. "You don't have to call home. My mom said she'd call for you."

"She shouldn't have to do that." Victoria waved her phone at her friend. "I'll make the call. How long does it take—thirty seconds?"

"It was easier this way." Hannah hiked counter-clockwise around the track. "Instead of arguing, just thank me so we can get to what's really important."

"Which is?"

"Using your power to help others." Hannah walked backward, facing Victoria. "I came up with a great idea in study hall."

Victoria wondered what Hannah and her mother would talk about. Would it have been limited to Victoria coming home late, or would they have spoken about how Hannah had gotten into more trouble since they'd become friends? The conversation could only end badly. Why didn't Hannah let her call home? A few extra seconds on their way to the track wouldn't have mattered.

"So what do you say?" asked Hannah.

"About..."

"You weren't even listening to me." Hannah slowed down. "Or did you change your mind about helping others?"

"I didn't change my mind. Just tell me again. I'll listen this time."

Hannah spun around to walk side-by-side with her.

"During our next gym class, you'll order Clare and Belle to stop teasing people. If they don't listen, you'll animate half their clothing to tear the other half apart. This way, no one gets hurt, and the popular girls won't bother anyone anymore."

"I'd never do that," said Victoria. "I'd be the center of attention."

"What's wrong with that? You'd be the most popular girl in school."

"Or the most feared."

A group of girls from the volleyball team joined them on the track, jogging in the opposite direction.

"We should try something more subtle." Victoria pulled Hannah off the pavement to avoid a collision with the athletes. "What if I animate their purses when no one is around? I can force their makeup to smear all over their clothing."

"They wouldn't know it had anything to do with their behavior. They might even think the boys played a prank on them. It's getting too crowded around here. I didn't realize anyone would run today."

Hannah led her toward the front of the school. "Late bus or walk home?"

"Let's walk," said Victoria. "So I can delay starting my homework as long as possible. A term paper is due soon."

"That's it. Can your creatures write?"

"I've never asked them to."

"There's always a first," said Hannah. "We'll let pens and pencils give them the message."

An opportunity presented itself a couple of days later. While Victoria was skimming through a book in study hall, Mina showed up with red eyes and sniffles. Earlier in the day, she'd seemed fine, so she'd either come down with a sudden cold or someone had upset her. It had to have been a popular girl, still upset about Mike's interest in a rival.

"What happened?" Victoria whispered.

"You were right." Mina wiped a tear off her cheek. "It didn't matter what I did. Clare and Belle were always going to find a reason to be mean."

"Did they hurt you? You should talk to the vice principal."

She couldn't believe she just said that. It was what her mother would have suggested.

"They didn't touch me," said Mina. "They're too fragile to risk a fight."

Victoria pulled her chair closer, making as little noise as possible. The teacher kept reading her book, oblivious to her students' problems. As long as it was quiet in the room, she was happy. Perhaps if teachers paid more attention, there would be fewer problems in school.

"They started a rumor," said Mina. "About Mike and me."

"You said you were going to turn him down."

"I did." Mina leaned closer and lowered her voice. "That's why they started the rumor about us making out. This way he wasn't rejected by a nobody, and I became the school slut."

"But you're not," said Victoria. "And your friends know the truth."

Or did they? Everyone kept secrets.

"Don't worry," she said. "In a week, no one will remember this."

"Thanks." Mina took out a book and some paper. "You're really nice."

Victoria was going to be more than nice. She was going to make sure no one talked about this rumor by giving them a more interesting topic to discuss. The popular girls had gone too far. She stuck her hand into her backpack and fished out a sharpened pencil. Clare and Belle were in Hannah's geometry class this period, only a few doors down.

"May I be excused?" asked Victoria. "I have to use the facilities."

She took the bathroom pass from the teacher's desk and headed down the hallway. When she reached the geometry room, she granted the pencil life and gave it detailed instructions, hoping it could carry them out.

The pencil creature sneaked into the room, hugging the wall. Victoria was glad she'd practiced a few times at home with varying degrees of success. Animating pencils was simpler than granting life to larger objects, but the creatures only kept track of a few commands at once.

A shriek from the classroom brought a smile to her face. Chairs scraped across the floor, voices grew louder, and the teacher shouted for order. Victoria wanted to peek inside but couldn't risk being spotted. Instead, she pressed up against the wall and waited. Eventually, the pencil creature wandered out the door. She picked it up, gave it a little kiss, and rushed back to study hall.

"Is everything okay?" asked Mina. "You were gone a long time."

"I think so." Victoria hid the pencil between her palms. "We'll see."

Mina gave her a funny look before returning to her work.

When it was safe, Victoria converted the creature back into a pencil and found a special spot for it in her backpack.

"I might have to call on you again," she whispered. "Sometimes people need a few lessons before changing their ways."

At the end of the period, Hannah showed up in the doorway and blocked Victoria from leaving.

"That had to be you," she said. "It was incredible."

A sense of pride welled up within Victoria. She couldn't wait to hear what had happened, even if it meant being late for her next class. Hannah pulled her aside.

"Belle screeched and threw a pencil across the room." She swiped at the air with her arm, mimicking Belle's motion. "'It's writing by itself,' she shouted. Half the kids jumped out of their seats, but no one knew what was happening. While they all stared at Belle, I moved between the pencil and the rest of the class to give it a chance to sneak away. Then she held up a piece of paper with writing on it. I couldn't read it because I was behind her, but everyone in front of her started laughing, including Clare."

"It should have read: Don't start rumors. What if everyone knew your mother sang you a lullaby to sleep every night?"

"Good one." Hannah chuckled. "Belle was so embarrassed she banged her shoulder against the door frame when she ran out of the room."

Victoria's good mood evaporated as her knees weakened.

"I didn't want anyone to get hurt." She fell against the wall.

"That wasn't your fault," said Hannah. "Belle should have waited until the bell rang and walked out with everyone else."

"But she didn't, and I keep hurting people with my gift. I better go or I'll be late for class."

Victoria hurried down the hall, wondering why she ever agreed to Hannah's plan.

Fewer kids loitered in the courtyard before school the next day. Perhaps the chilly weather convinced them to seek shelter, but those who remained outside whispered about Belle's breakdown. Victoria scooted past them to deal with her locker, once again piled up with papers. Hannah, who'd been quiet on the bus, kept her eyes averted, thankfully unwilling to revisit their recent argument about what was or wasn't garbage.

After the first bell rang, Brandon joined them.

"Watch out today," he told Hannah. "Lou and Mike are roughing up anyone who laughed at Belle. They're trying to find out who did this to her."

"Maybe she did it to herself," said Victoria. "Maybe she realized how mean she's been and couldn't hold back the guilt."

"You can try to convince those two," said Brandon, "but I doubt they'll listen."

"Or we can do something else." Hannah gave Victoria an inquisitive glance.

Victoria shook her head with a frown. What was she trying to do? Let Brandon in on their secret?

"Like what?" asked Brandon. "I can help."

"Like going to the vice principal," said Victoria. "With enough kids telling the truth about Lou and Mike, old squarehead will have to do something."

"You mean give them a detention," said Brandon. "They'll just come back meaner than ever. Detentions are only punishments for good kids. The rest view them as part of school life."

"If they hurt anyone, they'd get suspended."

Victoria had hurt other students, but she didn't mean to. "Let their parents come up with suitable punishments."

"You need more evidence than hearsay," said Brandon. "Even if you convinced twenty kids to turn them in, it would be one word against another."

"Then we'll get evidence," said Hannah.

The second bell rang, forcing them to race to class, but Victoria remained behind for an extra moment. She couldn't let Brandon become suspicious of her, yet she didn't want to let Hannah down. It would be difficult to use her ability to catch Lou and Mike, but it might help if she set a trap.

Near the end of gym class, Victoria complained of a stomachache and limped off the volleyball court. When she was out of sight, she sneaked into the boys' locker room and opened the lockers until she found Mike's clothes. This time, she didn't want to grant life to the shirt or pants. She wanted to affect the individual fibers, making them act like a gecko's feet. If successful, this would minimize violence yet still get the boys in trouble. It took several minutes of concentration, but eventually she was satisfied with her work. The mass of tiny creatures wouldn't remain alive for long, so she couldn't take any chances waiting for a confrontation.

Victoria found a piece of paper and a pencil in another locker and wrote:

Belle shouldn't have hurt Mina. She got what she deserved.
M

She shoved the note into Lou's locker, hoping Lou wouldn't question how it got there. Mike would deny writing it, but since he'd asked Mina out, Lou might not believe him.

The volleyball game hadn't ended by the time Victoria returned, but she couldn't focus on playing. She just avoided the ball when it came near her until the period was over. After she changed back into her school clothes, shouts emanated from the boys' locker room. A bunch of the kids spilled into the hallway, including Lou and Mike, who seemed ready to tear into each other.

"I told you it wasn't from me." Mike backed away from his friend. "Why would I put a note in your locker?"

"It doesn't matter," said Lou. "I bet you thought it was funny when Belle hurt herself."

"The note she wrote was funny. Nothing else."

When Mike turned away, Lou jumped forward and shoved him toward the wall. Lou's hand got caught in Mike's shirt, nearly causing both of them to fall over.

"Let go of me," said Lou.

"I'm not doing anything." Mike leaned backward to escape but pulled Lou with him. "You let go of me."

Lou sent his free hand flying at Mike, only to get caught in the shirt next to his other hand.

"Do you think this is funny, too?" Lou kicked Mike in the leg.

His foot became stuck near Mike's knee, forcing both of them onto the ground. The ruckus attracted the attention of both gym teachers, who quickly dispersed the crowd. Victoria, however, hung around, edging close enough to undo her work while remaining undetected.

Lou and Mike rolled away from each other and jumped to their feet.

"We weren't fighting." Lou handed the note to Ms. Macken. "Look what he wrote."

"You mean what someone else wrote?" said Mike.

"I don't care who wrote it." Ms. Macken crumpled the paper. "Fighting will not be tolerated in school. Both of you, to the principal's office."

"But—"

"Now." She tossed the paper into the trash. "And the rest of you, get to class. You're not little kids any more. Time to act your age."

Victoria turned and hustled away, satisfied that no one suspected her involvement.

Later that day, Victoria caught Brandon eyeing her near the hallway lockers. She ignored him, thinking he must have been looking at someone else, but after she swapped out some homework materials, he was still watching her. Had he tired of Hannah so quickly? He must have known Victoria would never go out with him if he dumped her friend.

"Can we talk?" he asked as he approached her.

"I'm not going out with you," said Victoria. "Do you really think I'd forgive you for cheating on Hannah?"

"No, I wasn't asking you out," he said. "I know... about you."

Hannah had told him! This was even worse than Brandon asking her out. Hannah had violated a sacred part of their friendship.

Victoria stared at Brandon, wondering what to do. She could deny it. If he never saw her use her ability, it would be her word against Hannah's. Besides, no one would believe them.

"What are you two talking about?" asked Hannah on her way to her locker.

"Why did you tell him?" asked Victoria. "It was my secret."

"Tell me what?" asked Brandon.

Victoria shut her locker and stepped back. If Hannah hadn't told him about her ability, how did he find out? Could he have been in the locker room with her? She had to learn more.

"Brandon has something to tell me," said Victoria. "But anything he wants to say, he can say to both of us."

He looked back and forth down the hallway. Most of the students had filed into the waiting buses, leaving them alone except for the occasional teacher.

"You're doing something," he said. "Every time there's a strange incident, you're always nearby. How do you make those things happen? Some type of magic trick?"

Victoria glanced at Hannah, who only shrugged.

"Yeah, just a simple trick," she said. "You wouldn't tell on me, would you?"

"Of course not," said Brandon, "but you have to show me how you do it."

"Another time." Victoria headed outside. "The buses are leaving soon."

Hannah followed her onto the bus and plopped down next to her.

"That was close," she said.

"Too close," said Victoria, "and it's not over yet. I still have to show him some trick or he'll become suspicious. I'm done."

"What do you mean?"

"No more helping people. It's too risky."

Hannah slumped back in the seat and stared out the window. Victoria didn't enjoy upsetting her, but if Brandon figured this out, so would others. It was only a matter of time before her secret came out and destroyed her life.

"Then we won't use your powers anymore," said Hannah, "but we can still help people."

"How? There's only the two of us."

"And Brandon. And Mina. And many others who are fed up with the teasing and shoving and rumors. Don't worry—I have a plan."

The next morning, Mike and Lou were back in form, shaking down anyone who might have known about the fake note. Victoria knew her deceit wouldn't last long, but she was glad it had worked. Unfortunately, Lou and Mike's detentions had no effect on their behavior, just as Brandon had predicted.

A crowd had gathered around them in the hall before homeroom as they cornered another helpless student. With the corridor blocked, Victoria wanted to find another way to class, but Hannah took her arm and marched straight through the group. Most of them separated on their own, but a few waited for Hannah to excuse herself before yielding. She made her way toward the bullied student, a boy Victoria didn't recognize, and grabbed his arm with her other hand.

"I was looking for you, Adam." She kept walking. "I need help with my Spanish homework."

Mike and Lou seemed too surprised to react, filling Victoria with confidence. Hannah, with no special ability, had accomplished what she couldn't. Arm in arm, they cleared the group of onlookers and continued down the hall, where Adam eventually detached himself from Hannah.

"You don't really need my help," he said. "Do you?"

Hannah winked at him and headed for her classroom.

"Thanks," he said with a nod.

Victoria knew they couldn't help everyone all the time, but perhaps others would learn from this example. One brave act could lead to another and another. Once enough students stood up to the bullies in school, everyone's life would be less stressful, except her own.

Chapter XVIII

Popularity

As the day progressed, Victoria felt more eyes on her. She wondered if Hannah was experiencing a similar situation, especially since she deserved the attention. Victoria had done nothing this morning except walk beside Hannah and Adam. At the beginning of the school year, she'd wanted a large group of friends, but a couple of close ones were much better. Too many people prying into your personal life was never good.

By lunch time, Victoria couldn't return any of the smiles coming her way. She kept her head down as she raced through the hallway to the cafeteria. Soon she'd bury her head in her food and ignore everyone else while she ate.

The odor drifting down the hallway caused her to slow from a run to a walk. It was curry day, overcooked rice smothered in an unidentifiable brown sauce. Victoria would have skipped the meal if she weren't so hungry and instead doubled up on milk, dry salad, and apples.

Hannah had already started eating when Victoria joined her at the table.

"Going vegetarian today?" asked Hannah.

"I don't know that I had a choice," said Victoria. "I can't tell if there's beef or chicken in the main dish. Either way, I've had enough of that slop to last me the rest of the year."

She dug into the salad, drowning out the bitter taste of lettuce with a swig of milk. Beside her, Hannah seemed to enjoy her meal, smiling back at each person who passed by the table.

"This is great," she said between bites of her sandwich. "Word has already spread about this morning. I expected it to take a few days."

"If you like this sort of thing," said Victoria.

"I thought you wanted to be popular. Isn't that why you bought clothes to match Clare's on the first day of school?"

"That was a mistake." Victoria pushed the rest of her salad aside and grabbed an apple. "And not because I forgot to take the tags off or because they were mean."

"Then why?"

"I'm not interested in being part of a group anymore." Victoria bit into the mealy apple. She spit the bite out into her napkin and shoved the tray to the center of the table. "I liked it more when it was just the two of us."

"Me, too," said Hannah. "But don't worry. We won't stop being friends because other kids want to hang around with us. It would take much more to break us apart."

How much more? Others learning about Victoria's power and calling her a freak?

Victoria finished eating early and headed to her English classroom. She wanted a few extra minutes to study before taking a quiz on the most recent chapters of *Pride and Prejudice*. After removing the book from her backpack, however, Clare and Belle strolled into the room, followed by their gang. Victoria would have ignored them, but they surrounded her desk.

"I'm not in the mood to fight," she said. "I just want to prepare for the quiz."

"We're not here to cause trouble." Clare took the seat next to her, while the other girls circled around. "Quite the opposite."

Victoria didn't believe her and tried to position her chair so all the popular girls were in sight. They were probably acting nice to play a prank on her, but she wouldn't let them. Whatever their motive, they weren't going to let her study.

"What do you want?" She tossed the book on her desk and crossed her arms.

"I'm having a party this Saturday," said Clare. "I was hoping you'd come."

"You want me at your party?" Victoria wasn't expecting anything like this. "After accusing me of ruining your clothes at Halloween?"

"I was upset about my new dress getting stained." Clare scooted closer. "I shouldn't have blamed you, especially since you and Hannah weren't near the table. The ladle must have slipped."

"And what about during volleyball? You thought I meant to give you that bloody nose."

Clare's smile fluttered but came back stronger than before. "That was an accident. It could have happened to anyone."

Did they figure out her involvement? Brandon's guess had been close. Luckily, he believed her when she showed him a simple card trick.

But why would the popular girls want her to go to a party, except to take advantage of her? If they knew about her ability, they were scared of her or wanted to control her. If not, they were planning a trick.

"It's no secret," said Clare.

They knew. Victoria gasped at a vision of people mobbing around her, making her life a zoo. They'd follow her home, hounding her until she had nothing left. Her worst nightmare had come true. Once the popular girls knew about her, everyone would. They'd never keep such an important secret.

"You and Hannah are popular now." Clare spread her arms. "You're one of us. Especially after the stunt you pulled off this morning."

Victoria let out a big breath. They'd figured nothing out. They only wanted to take advantage of Hannah's newfound popularity.

"There's no doubt you belong in our group. Isn't that right?" Clare glanced at her clique.

Belle and the others nodded back in unison. The group wouldn't have been more synchronized if they'd spent hours practicing. Disgusting. Victoria would never join them. She was even disappointed in her earlier self, trying to impress them with new clothes. How could she have been so naive?

Belle rubbed her arm where she bumped the door. Victoria regretted causing the injury and Clare's bloody nose. These girls, however, loved inflicting emotional pain. It might not have been physical harm, but it caused suffering. She doubted they ever regretted their actions. Why would she consider joining a group that hurt others to make themselves feel more important?

"Thanks." She reached for her book. "But I'm busy Saturday."

"Oh, too bad," said Clare. "What are you doing?"

Victoria hadn't expected her to pry further, but they didn't deserve an excuse. The other girls whispered to one another, probably shocked that anyone would turn down a party. They wouldn't believe her no matter what she said and neither would Clare, but she didn't care what they thought. She wanted nothing to do with them.

"I'll be sitting at home thinking how happy I am not being part of your nasty group."

Clare jumped off her seat, furious.

"I knew you caused that mess." She flicked her wrist at her posse to send them away. "You'll pay for what you did."

The gang dispersed, most heading to their respective classrooms, while a few took their seats in this class. Turning Clare down gave Victoria a deep sense of satisfaction as she sank into her chair and stared at the closed book in her hands.

Hannah entered the room a few steps ahead of the teacher and sat next to Victoria.

"What happened in here?" she asked. "Belle and the others didn't seem happy."

"They wanted us to join their group," said Victoria, "but I turned them down."

"Settle down, class." The teacher passed out a thick stack of paper. "Put away everything except your pencils."

Victoria shoved the book into her backpack. This would be difficult. She hadn't reviewed a single page, and thoughts of the popular girls planning their revenge occupied her mind.

Word must have spread that Victoria had stood up to Clare and the popular girls again. More eyes followed her down the hallway after each period until the entire school was watching her every move. She didn't wait for Hannah after the last period, and instead ducked onto the bus, slouching down in her normal seat.

Hannah soon joined her, sporting an enormous smile.

"Why'd you run off so fast?" she asked. "Doesn't it take extra time to juggle everything at your locker?"

"I don't like the attention." Victoria slumped down further. "And my locker's fine."

The bus bounced over the speed bumps and entered the busy road.

"There's nothing you can do about it now," said Hannah. "Just enjoy the attention while you can. No one else has stood up to them."

"Except you. Do you really like everyone staring at you all the time?"

"Why not?"

There were many reasons, but Victoria didn't want to ruin Hannah's mood. She gazed outside at the parting clouds, the sun desperately trying to break through.

A loud bang shook the bus, and they rolled to a stop on the side of the road. The bus driver peeked outside, explained that a tire had blown out, and returned to his seat to call a tow truck. Knowing they'd be stuck for a while, a few kids took out their books to study, but most went onto their phones.

"We can walk the rest of the way," said Hannah. "It's only a few blocks, and it seems like the rain is done."

Victoria followed her out, her spirits lifted by a ray of sunshine on her face. A hole had opened in the clouds, growing larger every minute. Just like she'd told Mina, this fascination with her would fade away after a few days, a couple of weeks at most. She only had to keep to herself and not use her ability.

As they approached her house, she stopped at the mailbox and reached inside. Along with the pile of catalogs and coupons for local stores, a letter from an attorney stood out. Victoria shoved it into her backpack.

"What's wrong?" asked Hannah. "What's that letter?"

"It's nothing." Victoria headed up the front walk. "See you tomorrow."

"It's not nothing," Hannah said from a few steps behind. "You're clearly upset about it."

"It's jury duty for my dad or something." She rushed to her door. "Don't worry about it."

Hannah turned toward her house. "Friends don't lie to each other."

She was right, but Victoria could barely hold back her tears.

Victoria woke up late and skipped breakfast to make the bus. She charged out of the house but stopped halfway down her walkway, where a curious smell forced her to turn around.

Egg yolks dripped down her front door and windows. Clare's gang must have thrown the eggs at her house early this morning. If the popular girls put as much effort into their schoolwork as they did trying to intimidate people, they'd be on the honor roll.

Victoria dropped her pack and rushed inside as the bus continued past. She had to clean the mess to avoid any confrontations with the neighbors, who seemed to stare out their houses more often lately. It only took a few minutes to wipe down the windows and door before Victoria started the trek to school.

First period was half over by the time she arrived at the front office. As she expected, the vice principal didn't care about her house. It might have been burglarized or have caught on fire, and he'd still expect her to be at school on time. He handed her a detention slip and sent her to class, where Clare and Belle smirked at her. She ignored them. If egging her house was all they had planned, it wouldn't be a bad day.

After class, the hallway seemed extra mobbed. Kids from every clique mulled around the lockers, including several popular girls who were uncharacteristically interspersed among the peons instead of clustered together. Victoria pushed her way through the mass of students, making certain to get to history on time, but Hannah stopped her.

"Why were you late this morning?" she asked. "I saw you from the bus window."

"I had to clean the eggs off my house," said Victoria. "Clare and Belle's brilliant prank."

"Couldn't it wait until after school?" asked Hannah. "Or couldn't your mom take care of it?"

"It's my chore."

"Really... one of your chores is cleaning eggs off windows? That's pretty specific."

She wasn't even trying to understand.

"Not just eggs," said Victoria. "Anything. I thought it would be a quick job. I didn't know I'd get to school so late."

"Right." Hannah's eyes lingered on her as they headed for next class.

After two steps, Hannah bent down, picked up an old geometry quiz, and handed it to Victoria.

"I wonder how that fell out." Victoria took the paper from her. "Strange."

She turned down the hallway but had only gone a few more steps when another student tapped on her shoulder.

"You dropped this." He held out a pencil.

At first, Victoria thought he was handing it over as an excuse to talk to her, but another pencil dropped out of her backpack while she was standing there. She snatched the pencil from him, picked up the one from the floor, and jammed them both into her backpack. They must have fallen out because it was too stuffed for the front flap to close properly. When she stepped away from the boy, the bottom of her pack tore apart, sending all of her papers onto the floor.

Victoria ignored the distant laughter, too busy picking everything up to care who it had come from. If Mr. Moritz caught her, he'd give her a few more detention slips to match the one she'd already received. She gathered everything into her arms and rushed to class, where she borrowed a stapler to repair her backpack. It wouldn't hold forever, but it would be strong enough to last the rest of the day.

She couldn't focus on schoolwork during class, thinking about her backpack. Clare and her gang had ripped it apart. They wouldn't get away with this, but she refused to risk her special ability becoming public knowledge. She'd have to rely on someone else to resolve the matter, someone with authority.

Before lunch, Victoria stopped by the front office to speak with the vice principal.

"Clare destroyed my backpack." She deposited the evidence on his desk. "What are you going to do about it?"

The corners of some papers poked through the holes, and the front flap was even farther from closing than before. Mr. Moritz examined the bottom, felt its weight, and pushed it back to her.

"You saw her do this?" he asked.

"No, but she was angry that I refused to go to her party."

"It looks like it was cut," he said, "but we don't know how it happened. We can't accuse people without proof. Anyone could have done this, or you might have rubbed against a sharp object by accident. One partial tear and the sheer weight of this would do the rest."

"I didn't lean against a knife," said Victoria. "So what am I supposed to do? Ignore the bullying?"

"You'll get a new backpack and use the opportunity to clean out some of this stuff." He nodded at the door. "You already know how I feel about clutter."

"What about Clare?"

"Our school does not tolerate vandalism or bullying. I'll make an announcement to address the situation."

On her way to the cafeteria, Victoria listened to his stern voice ringing throughout the corridor.

"It has come to my attention that one or more students might have been tampering with another student's belongings. You are all old enough to know better. Any violation of a fellow student's property will be dealt with strictly, including detentions, parental notification, and potentially police involvement."

His announcement wouldn't help, despite the threat of calling the police. Victoria would have to do something about it herself. She stormed into the cafeteria and chose whatever dish passed as food.

"You don't look happy," said Hannah.

Victoria showed her the bottom of the backpack.

"Clare did this, and no one cares."

"Ah, the vice principal's speech just now." Hannah sipped her water. "I wondered what had gotten him riled up. You shouldn't be surprised. We always knew he couldn't do anything without evidence."

"Forget evidence," said Victoria. "Clare and Belle will pay for this."

"They already have," said Hannah. "They're lashing out because you stood up to them. I bet they come for me later today or tomorrow."

She lowered Victoria's backpack to the floor and pushed the tray of food closer.

"So we won't do anything about it?" asked Victoria. "Just let them get away?"

"We're going to continue to stand up to them and inspire the rest of the students," said Hannah. "Their jealousy will only increase, and if they keep coming for us, it's only a matter of time before they're caught."

She leaned in closer.

"Besides, with everyone so focused on us, you can't risk doing anything... unusual."

Victoria couldn't argue. If she used her ability in school, somebody was bound to notice. She took a forkful of spaghetti, savoring the tangy tomato sauce. Let Clare and Belle dig themselves into a hole. What could they do that would be so bad? Slice up her backpack or ruin an old outfit. She could always sew a tear here or patch a hole there. Hannah had shown her how to be more mature, but would she ever learn this for herself?

Chapter XIX

Vermin

After English class, Victoria stopped at her locker to put away as much from her backpack as she could fit. Both lockers were already stuffed, having accumulated past assignments, new books, and other materials since her first detention. She wondered if the next detention would also be dedicated to organizing her belongings or if Ms. Fila would lecture her about why it was important to be prompt. Either type of discussion wouldn't help. Everyone should just leave her alone.

When she was done, her backpack weighed about the same as before, even after shoving a handful of papers into her locker. She leaned into the metal door with her shoulder to close it and noticed several girls gathering around her. Clare and Belle had positioned themselves on either side, and a cluster of sycophants fanned out into the hallway.

"It's terrible that someone messed with another student's possessions," said Clare.

"Is nothing sacred?" asked Belle. "Now I have to watch my backpack at all times."

"I wouldn't dare bring my good purse to school anymore." Clare smirked at Victoria. "Someone jealous of me might scratch it."

"I know it was you." Victoria jammed her backpack against the locker behind her back. "And I don't care. I'm not interested in any more of your drama."

"I don't know what you mean," said Clare. "I'd never touch someone else's belongings."

"Then someone in your gang did it." Victoria faced the popular girls. "None of you can think for yourselves. Is that what you want? To follow orders and be obedient for the rest of your miserable lives?"

"We do what we want," said Belle. "And we choose to be friends, unlike you, who have no other options. You and that freak, Hannah, have no one else."

So what if she was right? There was nothing wrong with having one close friend. Victoria didn't need a mob following her around and prying into her personal life. She didn't need anybody.

"Looks like she's about to cry." Clare sported a smug grin. "I guess she and Hannah aren't such good friends after all."

Victoria couldn't stand them anymore. Hannah might be mature enough to ignore their taunting, but she wasn't. One swift motion and she'd scare them enough to never bother anyone again. Did it matter if it ruined her life to help others avoid similar teasing? She raised her palm, ready to dole out justice.

"There you are." Hannah took Victoria's hand in hers. "I couldn't see you through this crowd. Let's go... class starts soon."

"Not yet." Victoria pulled away from her. "I'm still talking to Clare and her friends."

"Oh, yeah?" said Clare. "What else do you want to tell me?"

Victoria had more to say, but not to her. She could order her clothes to climb off her body or her purse to dump its contents. She could order their shoes to throw the entire group to the floor as she stood over them and laughed. They didn't know who they were teasing. Only a few inches away, Hannah stared at her with a furrowed brow, reminding her of the promise not to cause harm.

"Good luck on the geometry quiz." Victoria lowered her hand. "Let me know if you need help with the material."

Clare seemed stunned by the statement and could only manage a weak, "Thanks."

A simple look from Hannah had convinced Victoria to back down, whereas Clare's gang would have agreed with anything she did or said. Clare didn't have a true friend among the pack. They'd never speak to one another after graduation, other than reminiscing about their high school days at a reunion every ten years. Victoria, however, would remain close to Hannah throughout their lives, sharing stories and secrets all along.

Victoria slung her backpack over her shoulder and pushed through the girls, with Hannah at her side. Her anger toward the popular girls had turned to sympathy. They needed the attention because their lives were missing friendship. There was no point in giving up her secret over an old backpack and a few verbal barbs.

"Thanks for stopping me," she said to Hannah.

"It looks like you did it yourself," said Hannah. "What made you change your mind?"

"I finally understand what you told me. They'll destroy themselves one day, either by getting caught or by drifting apart. We'll just wait them out."

Each of Victoria's afternoon classes had assigned extra homework, including an important project in English and two more quizzes. She returned to her locker after the final bell to pick up the materials she'd need at home. As she stuffed it into her backpack, a couple of faint dings rose over the voices of the students rushing to the buses. It could only mean one thing. Staples were hitting the floor.

She wrapped her arms around the backpack just before the remaining staples popped out, causing the bottom to tear apart. Every paper, book, and pencil crashed onto the hallway floor. The staples had only been temporary, but why couldn't they have held until she got home, or at least until she got onto the bus? She wanted to scream, but any noise would alert the vice principal, always on the lookout for ways to reduce his stack of detention slips.

With a sigh, she bent down to pick everything up. If she didn't hurry, the bus would leave without her, forcing her to walk home through the chilly weather or wait for the late bus.

"We knew this would happen." Hannah knelt beside Victoria. "It's good today's Friday. You have the weekend to find a new backpack."

"Or I can sew this one," said Victoria.

Hannah collected the scattered pencils from the ground and wrapped them with a hair band.

"And go through this again when the seam rips? I'm not busy this weekend. I'll help you shop, and if you need extra cash–"

"I'll think about it," said Victoria. "First, let's clean this up before you-know-who wanders by."

She piled a few books together, but they collapsed when she turned around and knocked into them. Why now? She should have been more careful, but the situation had flustered her. Adam and Brandon stopped by to help, each one collecting half the books.

"We only have a few minutes before the buses leave," said Adam.

"How will you carry all this?" asked Brandon. "Your backpack's dead."

"It's not dead." Victoria held it close to her chest. "Only hurt, and I can heal it."

"Fine," said Brandon, "but you still need to get these books home without another spill. I don't know about yours, but my bus driver would never forgive you for making him late on his route."

"I don't care about the bus." Victoria held out her hand. "Give me the books. I need them this weekend."

"Take this." Mina offered her a tote bag. "I brought snacks for art class in this. You can return it next week."

"Thanks." Victoria deposited everything into the bag, including her backpack.

Clare couldn't have been more wrong. How many popular girls would risk missing their bus home for her or Belle? None of them. Adam, Brandon, and Mina hurried out as a group, but Victoria held Hannah back.

"Let's walk home," she said.

"In this weather?"

"Yes, isn't it perfect?"

Behind her, a late student darted through the hall to make the bus when he flew into the air and crashed onto the hard floor. He screamed in pain and held his leg. Victoria and Hannah hurried to his side to help, but a small object on the floor drew Victoria's attention. She picked up one of her old pencils that must have escaped notice when it fell out of her locker. By now, the nurse had been summoned and was helping the boy limp to the office. If it hadn't been for Victoria's messy locker, he would have been on his way home. She snapped the pencil in half and tossed it into the nearest garbage can before leaving the building with Hannah.

The rain held off until they reached Victoria's block, where they made plans for shopping on Sunday before parting ways. Hannah put her backpack over her head and dashed away, while Victoria strolled up her front walk. Next week, she'd be arriving home at the same time because of detention. It didn't matter. She wouldn't have changed anything about the past few days, other than the accident she'd just caused.

As she entered her house, she inhaled the scent of freshly baked bread and hearty beef stew. Plates and silverware clinked as her mother set the table. Her father and Eli would soon take their seats, ready for their evening meal together. Victoria dropped the tote bag beside the door and bounded upstairs with her backpack.

"I'll be down after I wash my hands," she called out. "Do we have a sewing kit?"

"I'll help you find it later," her mom yelled back. "The food's ready now."

Victoria's mouth watered. She tossed the backpack in her room and returned downstairs to find the dining room table set with their formal china, complete with wine glasses and silverware. When she was growing up, they always had a special meal on Fridays. Everyone in her family put their work aside to be together. Whether there were late meetings, after-school activities, or mounds of homework, the four of them would sit together to eat a home-cooked dinner discussing their hectic week.

Before today, the last time Victoria remembered a fancy meal at home was after midterms last year. She'd spent days studying for the tests, but they were so difficult she was sure she'd failed miserably. Her father told her not to worry about the grades. He considered it more important that she understand the material than garner a few extra points. Her mother gave her a second helping of dessert to make her feel better, but Eli's words still resonated in her mind.

"You're done with your tests," he said. "Now we can play again."

She'd never realized how much her company meant to him. Whenever something came up in her life, such as studying or hanging out with friends, she'd ignore him without a word, and he'd wait patiently until she was ready to be his big sister again. Why had she cared about those grades so much? She didn't even remember what she got on the tests, despite it only being a year ago.

Victoria managed a quick smile at the rest of her family before focusing on her place setting. Of all the silverware, only hers was everyday cutlery. She held up the stainless steel fork, splotched where the dishwasher had failed its rinse cycle.

"What's with this?" she asked. "It's not even clean."

Her mother placed a basket of biscuits on the table, took Victoria's fork, and swapped it with her own.

"Take mine if you prefer."

The other silverware must have gotten lost in the move. Victoria would search for it this weekend if she had the time.

Eli and her father dug into the biscuits, slathering them with butter, but she preferred to keep the bread plain when sopping up extra stew. Butter obscured the flavor too much. Her mother returned with a tray of stew, already portioned out. Victoria watched her mother set a ceramic bowl down in front of the other three place settings, but she received a plastic container.

"What is this?" Victoria pushed the food away.

"What's wrong, dear?" asked her mother. "I thought this was one of your favorite dishes."

"It was," said Victoria. "It is."

"Try it then," said her mother. "It's the same as always."

With a grumble, Victoria pulled the container back and dipped in her biscuit. It tasted no different from what she remembered. Perhaps most of the fancy dishes were still packed away. Yet another chore to occupy her time when she should be doing homework. She bit into the biscuit, savoring the tangy taste of onion and rosemary.

"It's delicious, Mom. Just what I needed after the disgusting cafeteria food."

"You can bring your own lunch to school," said her mom.

"I'd have to clear out space in my locker." Victoria dug into the dish with her fork. "Or get a bigger backpack. I don't feel like carrying two bags around school all day."

"Well, let me know what you decide. I'm happy to make you a sandwich or pack leftovers."

Victoria finished her serving and helped herself to another. After she found the china this weekend, they'd continue their Friday tradition with proper place settings for everyone.

Saturday morning passed quickly, between finishing the grocery shopping, helping Eli complete another level of his game, and starting her homework. Victoria shut herself in her room, trying to get as much done as possible to free up tomorrow for backpack shopping with Hannah. The more she dived into the details, however, the more it seemed she had to do. She opened her history book to read the next chapter when the doorbell rang.

Victoria sprang from her seat and raced out of her room. "I'll get it!"

Maybe Hannah had come to free her from schoolwork and bring her shopping a day early. She opened the door to find her neighbor, Mrs. Bailey, standing outside with a transparent plastic container under her arm.

"Are your parents home?" Mrs. Bailey craned over to peek past Victoria.

"They're not here." Victoria stepped forward to block her view. "But they'll be back later."

"They never seem to be around when I stop by," said Mrs. Bailey. "When will they get home?"

"I don't know. They went for lunch and a matinee. Can I help you?"

Mrs. Bailey held out the container for Victoria to see. The empty bin had a ragged hole in the bottom corner.

"Tell them about this when they get back," she said.

"What about it? It's an old plastic bin."

"With a hole bitten through it by a rat." Mrs. Bailey separated the top from the bin and waved both parts in the air. "We used to keep our cereal in here until the rat got into it, and there are more like it back home. We had to throw out half our food."

"What does your infestation have to do with my parents?"

"We never had a rat problem until you moved in."

Victoria was too busy to deal with her neighbor's issues. What did she think? They kept pet rats and let them out to roam the streets at night?

"At first we thought it might be a coincidence," said Mrs. Bailey. "So we set traps on all sides of our yard. Only the one near your house caught anything."

"That proves nothing," said Victoria. "Maybe you have rats that want to come here."

"It was enough to convince us," said Mrs. Bailey. "I'll give you one week to resolve this problem, or I'm reporting you to the health department."

Mrs. Bailey dropped the bin on Victoria's doorstep and stormed back to her house. If she thought a mess had attracted the rats, she should have known better than to leave garbage behind, empty bin or otherwise.

Victoria brought the container inside and slammed the door. Now there was even more work to do. She couldn't let Mrs. Bailey file a report. That would only attract more people, sniffing around for anything out of the ordinary. Even with her family involved, she'd need help to handle this situation.

She ran up to her room, closed the door, and returned to her book about Romulus Augustus. So much for her shopping trip tomorrow. She and Hannah had a much more important task to complete.

Chapter XX

Cracks in the Mirror

Victoria had stayed up late Saturday night doing homework. By midnight, the words on the pages had blurred and she couldn't concentrate. She drifted off to sleep with a book draped over her chest and a pencil in her fingers.

The smell of coffee and bacon roused her from her dreams far too early on Sunday morning. After rolling out of bed, she fished around for her book, eventually finding it buried under laundry on her desk chair. Somehow, it had made its way there from the bed. She must have put it away in the middle of the night and didn't remember.

The image staring back at her in the mirror was thinner than ever, probably because of the terrible lunches at school. After donning baggy sweatpants and a shirt, she headed downstairs, where her family had gathered around the kitchen table. The thick Sunday paper was piled in front of her father, separating his spot from the rest of the settings. Eli was hiding behind a box of his favorite cereal, and Victoria's mother was preparing another dish at the counter.

"I thought you might sleep all morning." She brought over a plate of waffles. "You were up late."

"I have a lot to do this weekend," Victoria said with a yawn. "Can I get a cup of coffee, too?"

"Since when do you drink coffee?" Eli peeked over his box.

"Since whenever I want," said Victoria. "Go back to your sugary mush."

Her mother opened the cupboard. "Let's see what's here."

She probably didn't want her to have any caffeine, but Victoria didn't buy any decaffeinated coffee in the past few weeks. What was the point? She wasn't drinking it for the taste.

"Forget it," she said. "I'll have juice."

As her mother poured her a glass, she drizzled maple syrup over the waffles and topped them with sliced strawberries. It wasn't her usual omelet, but with a side of bacon, it would give her enough energy to last the morning. Unfortunately, only a plastic bin of butter graced the center of the table. Victoria peeked at the stove, but there were no pans in sight. Her father and brother must have eaten all the bacon. Just her luck. If she hadn't had so much homework, she would have been up earlier. Next time she went shopping, she'd pick up an extra package so they wouldn't run out.

"Would you like another waffle?" her mother asked when she was almost done.

"Sure." Victoria stuffed the last bite into her mouth.

It was that or share her brother's disgusting cereal. She could almost hear the batter sizzling in the waffle iron. Her mother took a box out of the freezer and placed a solid disk into the toaster.

"What happened to the homemade waffles?" asked Victoria.

"This is all we have, dear," said her mom. "Don't you like them?"

"They're fine." Victoria took another scoop of strawberries.

The ding of the toaster startled her, louder than she remembered. Her mother slid the waffle onto a plate and sprinkled powdered sugar on top.

"I'm done," said Eli. "May I be excused?"

"Your sister's still eating." Victoria's mom brought over the waffle and removed the cereal box.

"It's okay." Victoria grabbed her plate and fork. "I have to get back to studying. I'll finish upstairs."

She poured syrup over the waffle and rose from her seat. "Hannah's coming over later."

"I'll clean up down here." Her mom gave her a smile. "Have fun with your friend, dear."

By the time she finished breakfast, Victoria only had an hour before Hannah arrived. She opened her book to continue reading, but a series of beeps emanated from her brother's room. He'd be lost without a computer, console, or handheld to play. Needing to focus on her school work, she banged on the wall.

"Keep it down in there," she shouted. "I'm reading."

The noise ended but returned to its normal level within five minutes.

"Hey." She pounded the wall again. "Can't you turn down the volume? I have another two chapters to go."

Again the pings stopped, but instead of silence, they were replaced by a persistent tapping. Was he trying to annoy her? It was nearly impossible to press keys so loudly. Victoria slammed her book onto her desk and marched next door.

"I told you I'm finishing my homework." She burst through the door into his room. "Enough noise."

Eli looked up at her from his bed, the game controller in his hands.

"I thought we weren't allowed in each other's room," he said.

Victoria wouldn't have cared about violating his space, but she didn't want him barging in on her whenever he pleased. She had to comply with their mutual agreement.

"Sorry." She stepped back into the hallway and knocked on the open door. "May I come in?"

"What's the password?"

"I don't know... please?"

"That's the magic word," said Eli. "You remember the password, don't you? From when we were little?"

She didn't have time for this, but she had to take away his game until she was done with homework. He could find a book to read or sit quietly and contemplate life. She glanced in his direction. His on-screen avatar had lost all its health, and he'd dropped the controller onto the floor.

"Oh, you can play your game," she said. "I'll read in the living room."

"You can't go down there." Eli sat up on the bed and displayed a mischievous grin. "The ground is lava."

"Then I'll jump from the stairs onto the sofa."

She peered at the staircase but couldn't see into the living room. It was too far for a single leap, but he might believe she could do it.

"Okay," he said, "but the lava's rising. There's only a minute before you have to find higher ground."

"Volcano." Victoria entered the room. "The password is volcano."

She was surprised he remembered their game from years ago. He couldn't have been older than six when they last played.

Eli beamed at her, ignoring his electronic device. She looked down at the blue carpet covering the floor.

"Uh oh." She leaped onto his desk chair. "I can't swim."

She rolled closer to him and jumped from the chair onto the bed.

"Phew. I made it, but now we're stuck in the middle of the ocean with nothing to eat or drink."

"What about this?" He removed a handful of cereal from his pocket.

Victoria wrinkled her nose as she snatched it away.

"Fish food." She scattered it across the floor. "If we had a net, we'd be all set."

Eli removed the cover from his pillow and handed it to her. She waved the pillowcase around the carpet and groaned as she brought the heavy load back up to the bed.

"There... that should be enough food for the rest of the day."

"I'm not eating raw fish."

"Don't worry," said Victoria. "I caught fish sticks and tartar sauce."

He laughed and pretended to eat some of it.

"I'll find a way home." Victoria hopped into the chair. "You keep a lookout for more ships."

"Aye, aye, captain," Eli said with a salute.

Victoria returned to her room but didn't feel like working. Instead, she grabbed supplies and headed back to Eli's room. Someone had to protect him from the pirate ship looming in the distance.

Eli would have played with Victoria all morning, but the alarm on her phone rang her back to reality. She'd set it for five minutes before Hannah was due. On her way out of his room, she returned the game controller and closed his door. He could make all the noise he wanted.

Victoria waited behind the front door until her friend's footsteps echoed outside.

"I assume this must be important." Hannah trudged up the walkway. "I don't normally get up so early on Sunday."

"Early? I've already had breakfast, read a book, and played with Eli." Victoria stepped aside to let Hannah in. "And I woke up late. Are you ready? We have a lot of cleaning to do."

Hannah raised an eyebrow at her on the way toward the sofa. She hopped onto the seat and draped her legs over the cushions.

"After our fight the other day, I told you I wouldn't help clean your room again," she said, "but I'll make an exception this time since you asked me so nicely."

"It's not my room," said Victoria. "It's the basement. Mrs. Bailey claims we brought rats with us, and I haven't been down there much since the move."

"What's wrong with rats? People keep them as pets."

"I know," said Victoria, "but if I don't do something, Mrs. B. will call the health department on us."

"Ooh, that sounds bad, but wouldn't it be better for your parents to handle this?"

"They're out for the day." Victoria hovered near the sofa, anxious to get started.

Hannah sat up and stared at her.

"Your parents are always doing something else when work needs to get done. If I were you, I'd suspect their motives. I suppose Eli's at a friend's house as usual?"

"No, he's in his room playing games."

She was becoming too inquisitive, but Victoria needed her help. Without her friend to help identify trash, she'd keep everything.

"We should ask him to help," said Hannah, "or at least say, 'Hi,' before we start."

"That would ruin his concentration. He's trying to beat some difficult levels. I'd rather finish the work ourselves. The sooner we're done, the sooner we can deal with my backpack."

Victoria nudged Hannah off the sofa. "Are you ready? There's a lot more to get through."

Hannah followed her downstairs, where cardboard moving boxes covered the floor.

"Wow," she said. "I thought the upstairs hall looked bad. Haven't you unpacked anything yet? You've been here three months already."

Victoria pushed a few boxes aside to make an aisle through the mess.

"We take out stuff whenever we need something, but that's not good enough for Mrs. Bailey. She wants every house on the block to be spotless, regardless if she's invited inside."

Hannah chose a box near the center of the basement and opened the top.

"Yup, it's definitely a rat."

She jumped back as a large rodent scurried out of a hole in the bottom and raced toward a dark corner. Victoria peered into the box. A couple of half eaten cereal containers lay amid piles of oat clusters, raisins, and wheat flakes... Eli's favorite food. How could he enjoy a bowl of cold, mushy grains instead of fresh eggs and bacon? She should give the rat to Eli as a pet. They had similar tastes in breakfast treats.

"I guess we forgot about this food. We can get rid of it now. Try another box."

"What if there are more rats down here?" asked Hannah. "I don't want to get bitten."

Victoria raised her palm toward the box of food and concentrated until it grew a set of arms and legs.

"Go find boxes with holes in the bottom." She pulled Hannah aside. "This guy will search for rats."

The box creature roamed around the basement, peeking at its inanimate brethren. Whenever it found another chewed up corner, it raised its hand. By the time it returned to normal, it had discovered three rat holes. Victoria opened one of the damaged boxes, prompting a second rat to jump out and scurry away.

"This isn't a simple rat problem," said Hannah. "We should call an exterminator."

"I thought vegetarians didn't harm animals," said Victoria.

"Okay then, call someone to trap and release them." Hannah moved toward the stairs. "We can't do much cleaning until they're gone. It's too dangerous."

"Sure we can," said Victoria. "There's only a few boxes with holes. We'll just move them aside."

"And then what? There's still an infestation down here."

"We need something fast to catch them all."

She opened a few intact boxes until she found a partially deflated basketball. After granting it life, she commanded the spherical creature to chase the rats. The ball rolled around the basement behind her as she kicked each of the bitten boxes. Eventually, another rat leaped out of the hole. With the ball in close pursuit, they raced from one corner to the other.

The ball stopped below a bright light and seemed to deflate further. Victoria inched closer to a small hole in the outer wall. A few cables ran from outside, through the hole, and into the ceiling. The rat had escaped, but if they scared the rest of them and plugged the hole, the problem would be solved.

"I know how they're getting inside." She cleared a path from the stairs to the hole. "Start piling the good boxes on the other side and guard them. We'll scare the rats out of the basement."

She patted the ball creature. "Good work. Only a few more to go."

Over the next several minutes, they drove five more rats out of the house. Victoria returned the ball creature to normal and found some small stones outside to seal the hole.

"Are you satisfied?" she asked when she returned.

Hannah paced around the basement and approached her with a tentative smile.

"For now," she said, "but one more rat and I'm going upstairs."

"Didn't you tell me some people kept them as pets?"

"Yeah, some people... but not me... and certainly not wild rats."

"Fine," said Victoria. "Let's get started. I brought these from the kitchen."

She tossed a roll of heavy duty garbage bags to Hannah.

"Are you sure you're ready to throw things away?" asked Hannah. "Last time we got into a terrible argument."

"That was before I hurt a boy in school last Friday. If it's trash, it can go. I'll find a place for the rest of it in the house."

Hannah opened the nearest box and pulled out a frying pan.

"Kitchen." She handed it to Victoria.

"We already have more pans than we need," said Victoria, "but I'll find a spot in the cabinets upstairs."

Hannah grunted as she lifted the box.

"I'll help you," she said. "It'll go faster."

"No, you were right before." Victoria took the box from her. "Organizing kitchen utensils is a job for my parents. I'll leave this box for them in the kitchen. Keep working. I'll be back soon."

She brought the box upstairs and deposited it on the table, staring at the empty stove top for a moment before returning downstairs. Hannah had opened another couple of boxes containing women's clothing.

"These look like your mom's," she said. "Does she need them?"

Victoria pulled a dress out of the box. Her mom had worn it to an anniversary party two years ago.

"My mother can decide what to do with these." She carried the box toward the stairs.

"We'll be done in no time the way this is going." Hannah grabbed the second box of clothes.

"Just put it on top of this one." Victoria lowered her box.

"Why? I can bring this one upstairs."

"We're making good progress with you searching and me putting them where they belong." Victoria shook her box. "They're not heavy."

She blocked the stairway until Hannah yielded. The two boxes together weighed more than she expected, but she took one step at a time and returned quickly. Hannah had found another box of kitchen utensils and silverware.

"If you want a break from the basement," Victoria said as she caught her breath, "you can put that one on the kitchen table with the first one we found."

"I'm good." Hannah moved to another box. "Have fun going up and down the stairs all day."

Victoria brought it to the kitchen, wondering where everything would fit. This house should have more space than her previous home, yet they kept finding more boxes of clothing and gadgets. Both Hannah and Mrs. Fila had given her excellent advice, which she ignored until today. She could throw things away and get along fine.

Downstairs, Hannah had gathered three more boxes near the stairs.

"These are full of men's clothing." Hannah held up an expensive suit. "After my dad died, all his clothes would have fit into two boxes, but these all seem to be your father's."

"So my dad owned more outfits than yours did," said Victoria. "Not all men get by with a few pairs of shirts and jeans."

"I suppose not," said Hannah, "but this stuff looks freshly pressed and folded."

"What about it?"

"My dad never had his clothes pressed unless he was going to a special event. He'd always rush to the cleaners the day before to get his shirt and suit ironed."

Victoria closed the box and picked it up.

"Well, my dad works at home. He doesn't need suits anymore."

After she deposited the next few boxes in their proper rooms, she suggested a lunch break.

"Should I call Eli down?" asked Hannah.

"He'll eat when he's hungry," said Victoria, "but let's make a sandwich for him, just in case."

She led Hannah to the kitchen, moved the boxes from the table to the floor, and got out the supplies for peanut butter and jelly. As she prepared the bread, she kept staring at the boxes. She couldn't believe how many had been left downstairs.

Chapter XXI

The Truth

After lunch, Victoria and Hannah headed downstairs to fill garbage bags with the loose food. When they were done, Victoria took the bags out to the trash, while Hannah broke down the cardboard boxes for the recycling bin. Within the hour, they could see the entire basement floor.

"What are you going to do with all this extra space?" asked Hannah.

"Maybe my dad will set up a workshop down here," said Victoria, "or a home office."

"Where does he work now?"

"Mostly in the kitchen or the living room." Victoria hopped onto the first stair. "How about helping with my room next?"

Hannah grabbed the roll of trash bags. "You sure you're ready?"

"Why not? After doing such a great job down here, I know we can succeed."

She led Hannah to her bedroom, where clothes and cardboard boxes covered everything, including the chair, the desk, and the bed. On her own, it didn't seem so bad, but with her friend behind her, she realized how messy it was.

"This is worse than last time," said Hannah. "What have you been doing? Redecorating with litter?"

"So it's not as clean as your room. Are you going to help me or just complain?"

"Sorry." Hannah waded through the mess. "Let's sort through the boxes first. We had good luck with them in the basement."

"Are you being sarcastic?"

Hannah stared into her eyes. "I'm serious. I'm here to help you."

She tore open the nearest box and dug into a pile of artwork. "This looks like kid's drawings."

"Yeah... from Eli and me when we were younger."

Hannah piled it near the door.

"This just takes up space. You should snap photos of what you want to remember and recycle the rest. No need to fill your room or any other part of the house. It's not like you're going to frame any of it."

Victoria picked up the top picture, a stick figure drawing of four people, a house, and a flower garden. She snapped a photo with her phone but couldn't put the picture back on the pile. Instead, she cleared a small space for it on her desk.

"I might frame it." She shoved her books aside to give the drawing more room.

Hannah unrolled two trash bags, filling one with the stack of papers from the doorway.

"These are for trash and recycling." She grabbed the picture from Victoria's desk. "You're not framing a drawing from second grade."

Victoria snatched the picture back and compared it to the snapshot on her phone. Other than the size, they appeared the same. Getting rid of the physical copy didn't mean she wouldn't be able to look at it again. She glanced at her friend, who stood with a frown, waiting for the picture. Victoria handed it back to her.

"What about this?" Hannah removed a piece of cardboard with macaroni glued onto one side.

"It's me." Victoria smiled as she took the artwork from Hannah and held it up to her face. "Eli made it at camp a few years ago. He said he missed playing with me and created the mask for one of his friends to wear."

She glanced at the wall between her room and his. Silence. Maybe he'd finished all the levels and was done with the game. It wouldn't be long before he found another one to play.

"You know the drill," said Hannah. "Take a picture of the mask and place it in the bag."

"But this isn't just a simple drawing," said Victoria. "He spent a full day gluing each piece of pasta in the right position."

"And you'll always have a reminder of his work. You can look at the photo any time you want. It's even better than having the original packed away at the bottom of a forgotten box in the basement."

Victoria took a photo but held the mask in her hand. Keeping one piece of art wouldn't be bad. Hannah nodded, giving her the strength to place the mask in the trash bag. Without her friend, she couldn't have done any of this, yet she still fought to hold back the tears.

"Shall we continue?" asked Hannah. "Or do you need a few minutes?"

"What else is in there?" Victoria wiped her eyes.

Hannah gazed into the box with a worried look. It must have been something with even more sentimental value, but Victoria couldn't imagine what her friend had found. She dreaded peeking as Hannah tilted the box toward her. It was empty.

"One down." Hannah's bright smile lifted Victoria's spirits. "That wasn't so bad, and only three more to go. Then we can take a break before tackling the rest of this disaster."

Victoria didn't need to rest. She wanted to get through the day. Hannah tore the sides off the box and tossed them into the bag for recycling. What once had felt like an impossible task was now a step closer to completion, thanks to her best friend.

It took an hour to go through the rest of the boxes, snapping photos of memorable art projects. They'd filled two bags of trash and one for recycling, not including the torn cardboard. Victoria gathered all three bags and stepped into the hallway.

"I'll be right back," she said. "You can get started with the clothes. Anything with holes or stains can be thrown away."

"Are you sure you trust me with your clothes?" asked Hannah. "Why don't you stay here, and I'll take the bags out."

"I can't toss anything on my own. You should know that already."

"I suppose." Hannah pushed a few outfits off the chair to sit down. "Go ahead. I got this."

Victoria lugged the bags downstairs and out the door, where she was stopped by Mrs. Bailey in her yard.

"Is your mom or dad home?" she asked on her way over.

"They're out for the day," said Victoria, "but I already started cleaning up. See? All getting tossed into the bin."

Mrs. Bailey tromped up the walkway, eyeing the front door. Victoria moved backward to block her view.

"We saw rats running around your yard in the middle of the day," said Mrs. Bailey. "We're not waiting to call the health department. Something has to be done before they spread disease throughout the neighborhood."

"It should be better now," said Victoria. "They were getting into my house through the hole for our cable lines. I chased them out of the basement and plugged the hole. Since they can't get back inside anymore, they'll have to find a new home. You've seen the last of them."

"Do you mind if I check for myself?" Mrs. Bailey pressed forward, peering through the open door. "A second set of eyes might discover another entry point."

"My parents will help when they get back. Besides, they don't like anyone else in the house when they're not home."

"What about your friend? I saw her come over a couple of hours ago."

"Hannah?" Victoria peeked over her shoulder into the house. "She's more like a sister. What were you doing anyway... spying on us?"

Mrs. Bailey stepped to the right, but Victoria kept in front of her. She was too curious. Victoria dropped the bags on the stoop and slammed the door shut.

"We weren't spying on anyone," said Mrs. Bailey. "We were raking leaves when your friend passed by. Hannah seems like a nice girl... it's so sad about her father."

Victoria folded her arms across her chest.

"I'll trust you this time." Mrs. Bailey stepped backward. "But one more rat and it's over. No more delays."

"Okay."

Victoria picked up the bags as her neighbor headed home.

"And one more thing," Mrs. Bailey said from the end of the walkway. "I should have met your parents by now. Tell them to call me as soon as they get home. We're getting together this week. I'll adjust my schedule to fit theirs."

Why did she have to cause trouble? Some people were too busy to hang out with neighbors all the time. As long as they didn't bother one another, everything should have been fine.

Victoria brought the bags to the side of the house and jammed them into the bin. She threw all her weight onto the can to close the lid. The garbage collector would probably wonder why there was so much trash this week, but it couldn't be too unusual. A single party would easily double the amount of waste coming from a family.

When Victoria returned to the front of the house, she found the door locked. She'd forgotten to unlock it when she was speaking with Mrs. Bailey, and the key was in her room with Hannah. She rang the doorbell twice, but no one answered.

"Hannah!" She rapped on the door. "Open up. I locked myself out. Can you hear me?"

A flurry of footsteps came from inside, and Hannah opened the door.

"Eli's not in his room," she said. "I thought he'd answer the doorbell, but when you called my name, I checked on him."

"Oh, he might have gone to his friend's house," said Victoria. "Don't worry about him."

"If he were my little brother, I'd be more concerned."

"He's fine," said Victoria. "Let's finish cleaning, unless you have something better to do."

Why couldn't everyone stop asking questions and let her live her life?

"No, I have nothing better to do than spend my day off cleaning someone else's house." Hannah winked at her. "I was only concerned about your brother, but if you say he's fine, I believe you."

She returned to the bedroom, with Victoria close behind. Most of the clothing had been thrown into the corner with a single trash bag lying half full nearby.

"I only found a couple of damaged items." Hannah waved a hand in front of her nose. "The rest should go into the laundry."

"I'll bring it there now," said Victoria.

"By the way, when's laundry day around here? My mom does a load every other day, and it's only the two of us. I'm surprised your washing machine isn't running round the clock."

"We do the wash enough to be sick of the chore."

Victoria grabbed the clothes and dumped them into the bathroom hamper, returning to an unfamiliar sight in her room. Other than a few wisps of lint and little scraps of paper, the floor appeared clean. She didn't remember seeing this much carpet since she moved in.

"Thanks for the help," she said. "We're done, and there's still a few hours left in the day."

"Not yet," said Hannah. "Your desk is still a mess."

"Don't worry about it. I'll organize those papers later."

"Nonsense." Hannah grabbed a sweater off a pile of school books. "We've come this far together. We might as well complete the chore."

She tossed the sweater aside and reached for a stack of papers.

"I'll get those." Victoria lunged forward and knocked into the pile.

Papers flew off the desk and scattered onto the floor, including one unopened envelope.

"What's that?" Hannah bent down to retrieve the letter. "Is this what upset you the other day?"

Victoria tried to snatch the envelope away.

"It's not for your dad." Hannah stared at the addressee. "It's for you, and it's from a lawyer. I don't understand. What's going on?"

"Give it back." Victoria held out her hand. "It's none of your business."

Hannah turned away from her and broke the seal.

"That's illegal," said Victoria. "You can't open someone else's mail. You'll go to jail."

She jumped at Hannah, but her friend only held it closer to her chest. Victoria stretched forward but couldn't get it back before Hannah removed the letter from the envelope.

"DON'T!" Victoria screamed.

Hannah opened the letter and held it away from Victoria as she read through it. Her fingers trembled as she handed it back.

"Why would you be called as a witness to a vehicular manslaughter trial? That would mean..."

Victoria shoved the letter under her books and kicked the empty envelope behind her desk.

"You should go now," she said. "I told you I'd take care of this."

"Were you in an accident?" Hannah's eyes widened. "Where are your parents?"

"I already told you they went out today."

"Where?" Hannah grabbed her shoulders and faced her. "Exactly where did they go? Which restaurant? Which movie? When will they be home?"

Victoria glanced through her doorway, falling to her knees when Hannah finally let go. She felt sick. Her stomach turned as her heart beat faster.

"Just go home," she said weakly. "Everything's fine the way it is."

"It's not fine," said Hannah. "Stop lying to me! I'm not going anywhere until you tell me the truth."

Why did she keep pressing? Who cared about the truth?

"Please forget about it," said Victoria. "I'll do anything. I'll use my power whenever you want... even in school. We can go to your house now and finish our homework together."

Hannah ignored her plea as she stepped out of the room and peered down the hallway. Clearly she was hesitant about learning any more. Victoria lifted herself up and stumbled after her. Even if she could stop her friend, she wasn't sure if she wanted to. Hannah wouldn't believe any more lies, and Victoria couldn't live without their close friendship.

They inched down the hall toward the closed door at the end. There was still time to turn around, but Hannah reached forward and turned the knob. Tears streamed down Victoria's face as she sank to the floor against the wall, turning her head away from the creaking door. She didn't have to look inside the room to know what was there: her parents and Eli standing near the master bathroom, their scarred faces staring back at Hannah.

"No!" Hannah staggered backward. "It can't be. Not all of them..."

Hannah's flood of tears matched Victoria's as she collapsed in the hallway. Victoria buried her head on Hannah's shoulder.

"They all died in the accident," she said eventually, "but I brought them back to life."

"What?" Hannah wrapped her arms around Victoria. "How?"

"Child services was going to put me in a foster home with strangers. I sneaked into the morgue, animated my family, and forged some papers, supposedly transferring their bodies to where my grandparents were buried. I couldn't live in the same town anymore, so I sold our old house and bought this one after forging more documents. It was going well until people kept asking too many questions."

"Going well?" asked Hannah. "This is no way to live."

"But they're not dead anymore. I can keep them alive as long as I want."

"You can't go on like this forever." Hannah held Victoria tightly. "I'm so sorry about what happened, but you have to let them go. They wouldn't want this."

"I can't. I don't want to be alone."

Hannah shifted to the front and held her hands.

"You will never be alone," she said. "I promise."

Victoria wiped the tears from her cheek as she gazed past the door into her parents' room. Were they really alive? Or were they pretending to be her family? Hannah was right. She couldn't force them to live out her fantasy. They deserved peace.

"I love you," she said. "Goodbye."

Three thumps brought another round of tears she couldn't stop. Hannah pulled her close, reassuring her that everything would be fine, but Victoria didn't think she'd ever stand again. Her family was gone.

CHAPTER XXII

SISTERS

Victoria missed school the next few days as she prepared for a private funeral with help from Hannah's mother. She wished Hannah could have skipped school because Mrs. Walton wasn't happy learning about Victoria's special ability. Planning sessions for the funeral were separated by long stretches of awkward silence between them.

"If it makes it easier, we can tell everyone the truth," said Victoria. "You and Hannah have been so kind to me. I don't want to force you to keep my ability a secret. It's too much of a burden."

"The truth would make things worse," said Mrs. Walton. "The questions, the publicity, not to mention the possibility of you becoming a lab rat in some government facility. Although you've had to grow up quickly, you're still a child. Give me time to get used to your unique talent."

"Would it help if I never animate anything when you're around?"

"It might. Maybe one day I won't be as bothered by it. Either way, you're welcome in our home, but I'm not sure how we'll make it official. Questions will be asked."

"I might have forged a few papers with the help of my power." Victoria gave her a hopeful look. "Officially, I'm emancipated."

"That only works when your parents are alive."

"Thankfully, nobody looked into it too deeply."

Mrs. Walton seemed relieved as she returned to the preparations.

An icy wind blew on the day of the funeral. Victoria shivered under the gray sky, pulling her black coat tighter around her body. Hannah and her mother stood nearby, with a small crowd behind them. Most friends and acquaintances lived in Victoria's old town, but she couldn't have gone there for the service. Too many questions would have been asked.

Three mounds of dirt sat beside three deep holes. Victoria tried not to peer down but couldn't help herself. At the bottom of the holes lay the caskets with bouquets of calla lilies decorating each one.

Hannah and her mother put their arms around Victoria, infusing her with warmth.

"We're here with you," said Hannah.

On the other side of the graves, the funeral director had been speaking for several minutes, but Victoria hadn't listened. She'd given him notes about her family because she couldn't deliver the speech. It was difficult enough to remain standing. Eventually, the director held out a shovel for her. She glanced at Hannah, who nodded back. This was it, sending her family away forever.

Victoria jammed the shovel into the pile of dirt and heaved a big scoop into the first hole. The pebbles clattered against wood, causing a flood of tears to pour down. She moved to the second hole, repeated the process, and finished at the third grave.

Her legs wobbled, forcing her to steady herself with the shovel. She couldn't do this alone. Mrs. Walton came forward to support her, while Hannah sent a few shovelfuls of dirt into the graves. The funeral director waved at the guests, allowing them to form a short line behind Hannah.

Mrs. Bailey came first, skipping the shovel.

"I'm sorry for your loss." She offered Victoria a firm hug. "I'm here for whatever you need."

Her husband followed with similar sentiments, but Victoria could only hear the dirt piling up in the graves as each person had their turn with the shovel. When the rest of the neighbors had passed, the coffins were no longer visible, only three partially filled holes.

Hannah tugged on Victoria's arm, but she wasn't ready to leave. She waited until the workers had flattened out the three piles, leaving no trace of her family other than brown patches in a field of grass and tombstones. Victoria fell to her knees and cried, wondering why something so horrible had happened to her family.

Long after everyone else had left, Victoria took the bus home, against Hannah's wishes. Mrs. Walton wanted to drive her, but Victoria wasn't ready to ride in a car yet. Although the bus seats were packed, she felt alone. One side street after another passed by the window, blending together into a single gray composite.

When the bus drove through a tunnel, her face stared back at her in the glass. She tried to recall her parents and Eli without the terrible scars but only saw them walking around the house, pretending to be alive. She'd been selfish to force them into a partial existence, but it didn't matter anymore. They were at rest now.

After the bus turned onto her street, a flash of bright red caught her eye. Hannah had thrown a colorful coat over her somber clothing and was waiting outside. She jogged next to the bus until it stopped at the corner, depositing Victoria onto the sidewalk.

"Just because you refused our ride," she said, "doesn't mean you can refuse my company."

"Thanks." Victoria dried her eyes and gave her friend a weak smile. "There's not much left to pack, but I could use help."

She was glad she was moving in with Hannah and her mother. Living on her own would have been unbearable. It had been hard enough to get by with her reanimated family keeping her company.

The drawn window shades made her house appear to be asleep. Victoria preferred not to disturb it, but she had to pick up the last of her belongings. She opened the front door and led Hannah inside.

No boxes cluttered the living room floor, and no knickknacks dotted the shelves. The dining room was similarly empty. Victoria didn't have to pack anything from those two rooms. They'd been bare since she moved in during the summer. The kitchen only held a few items other than the boxes Victoria and Hannah had brought up from the basement. Some forks and knives lay in their drawer, and scattered food items hid in the cabinets.

Victoria removed four packages of frozen waffles from the freezer and dumped them in the garbage. She'd had enough of them for a while. A similar fate awaited the jars of peanut butter and jelly on the refrigerator door.

"This is one good thing about not unpacking," Hannah called out from upstairs. "There's not much to do before you can move in with us."

"All the clothes and most of the boxes can go to charity." Victoria joined her in the hallway. "I already put my favorites into a suitcase."

"Are you sure?" asked Hannah. "We have room to store things downstairs."

"I wouldn't want to lure any rats into your basement."

Hannah allowed a single chuckle to escape her lips before she grabbed the nearest box and carried it out the front door, where her mother's car awaited. She'd promised to make as many trips as necessary to donate the clothing.

Victoria wandered into her bedroom and stood beside the bed, its covers crumpled near the bottom. She raised her palm at the pillows, granting them life.

"Straighten up this mess," she said. "You want to impress the new owners, don't you?"

The pillow creatures marched down the mattress, grabbed the top sheet, and pulled it taut. They repeated the motion with the comforter, the creases in their pillow cases almost making it look like they were smiling.

"I'll come back for you after the house is sold." Victoria returned them to normal.

"Who are you talking to?" Hannah asked when she returned.

Victoria glanced at the pillows to answer her question. She grabbed her suitcases and headed downstairs, ready for her new home.

That night, the aroma of tomato, basil, and garlic filled the house. Hannah had set the kitchen table with everyday plates, forks, and glasses, but it appeared fancier than a formal ball to Victoria. She should have worn more than a pair of torn jeans and an old sweatshirt, but Hannah sported a matching outfit, making her feel more comfortable.

Mrs. Walton brought in a dish of steaming lasagna, straight from the oven. Victoria would have eaten the whole thing, but she noticed how Hannah also gazed at the food. She'd never impede her friend's happiness, not by hogging all the special lasagna and not by interfering with her and Brandon.

"Serve yourselves." Mrs. Walton returned to the kitchen for a tray of fresh garlic bread.

Hannah scooped out a slice of lasagna and placed it on Victoria's plate, followed by a large helping for herself.

"Don't get used to this," she said. "Tomorrow, it'll be back to normal meals."

"After months of frozen food and sandwiches," said Victoria, "I'll love anything your mom cooks."

"Tell me that in a few months." Hannah smiled and dug into her meal.

Victoria savored every bite of the delicious dinner. She'd say the same thing tomorrow, next week, and any day in the future. She was sure of it.

"I hope no one goes back to the old newspapers." Mrs. Walton took her seat and handed out the garlic bread. "They might find the article about the real accident and start asking questions."

"Eli's and my name never appeared in the paper," said Victoria. "It would be difficult to trace last year's accident back to me."

"But this supposed accident never made the local papers," said Hannah. "Some people will find it strange... like Brandon. He was already getting suspicious."

"He might wonder what really happened." Victoria finished her serving and took another. "But I'll tell him I asked for this tragedy not to be publicized because of my brother's age. It's almost what happened last year."

"That's not the way it works, but I hope he'll believe it," said Hannah. "Otherwise we'll be answering plenty more questions."

Hannah reached for the serving spoon.

"Victoria might like the rest of the lasagna for lunch tomorrow," said her mom.

"There's no microwave at school," said Hannah. "No one likes cold lasagna."

"I don't mind it, but it's too much for one serving. You should take half."

"You shouldn't suffer cold lasagna for lunch." Hannah scooped out her portion and glanced at her mother. "Let's save the rest of it for dinner tomorrow."

"And suffer through another disgusting cafeteria meal?" asked Victoria. "No thanks."

"Or you can have a peanut... oh... never mind."

She took a sip of water, possibly to cover her red cheeks.

"Any homework left for tomorrow?" asked Mrs. Walton.

"Mom, we're not in elementary school anymore."

Her mother stared at her.

"Fine," said Hannah. "A little more."

"Then I'll clean up down here," said her mom.

"I'll help." Victoria cleared the dishes from the table and loaded them into the dishwasher.

If this were the cost of living with her best friend, she'd gladly pay the price every day.

After the kitchen was clean, Victoria went upstairs to her room. Hannah's mother had given up her home office and bought a new bed for Victoria. Her school work was piled neatly on the desk, and not a single item of clothing littered her floor. She was sure the room wouldn't remain this organized for long, but she swore not to let it get as bad as in her house.

Hannah knocked on the door and stepped in, holding a blanket and a pillow.

"I thought you might want some company tonight." She placed her stuff on the floor. "I'll camp out here."

"I was getting lonely," said Victoria.

"Remember, my mom and I are always around if you want to talk." Hannah sat in the desk chair and rolled closer. "But if you want someone else..."

"There's always your therapist," said Victoria. "I know. One day I'll be ready to talk to her about the accident."

"Or anything else."

Hannah patted the comforter and nodded at the pillows on the bed.

"These corners are pretty tight," she said. "We might not be able to loosen them on our own."

With a smile, Victoria brought the pillows to life and ordered them to pull the bed sheet down. They complied with the command and stood at the foot of the bed with their little arms crossed.

"I think they want more to do," said Hannah.

"Wow. Usually I could only manage a single task before tiring. Now I can keep them alive all night."

Victoria pointed at Hannah's blanket. "Make her bedding more comfortable. She's staying with us tonight."

Her pillows jumped off the bed, straightened Hannah's blanket, and fluffed her pillow before awaiting their next task.

"You must have been concentrating so much on your family," said Hannah, "that you couldn't properly control the other creatures you animated. Just think what you can accomplish."

Victoria imagined experimenting with the limits of her power in the future, but for now, she was content to spend time with her new family.

The End

Legends of the Four Races

The Legacy of Ogma by E. A. Rappaport **978–0–9789393–0–4** **292 Pages $12.95**	The thief wants riches. The knight wants justice. The warrior wants a good battle. The sorcerer wants power. Each adventurer carries a mysterious crystal sphere that will lead to a long-hidden secret beneath the sea.
Forging Paradise by E. A. Rappaport **978–0–9789393–2–8** **306 Pages $12.95**	After a supposedly mythical race of desert warriors invades the human territories and destroys every city in its path, five former enemies must travel together into the netherworld and harness the unpredictable power of demons to defeat the seemingly invincible army.
Shadow from the Past by E. A. Rappaport **978–0–9789393–4–2** **282 Pages $12.95**	Mysterious fires fan an ancient grudge between Arboreals and Ferfolk, pushing lifelong enemies toward a devastating war. Two young strangers must overcome their mutual mistrust and uncover the real force threatening to ravage the land.
Secrets of the Undercity by E. A. Rappaport **978–0–9789393–3–5** **308 Pages $12.95**	Abandoned and betrayed as a child, Halia seeks revenge. Frustrated by his limited abilities, Oswynn seeks powerful magic. The paths of the thief and apprentice cross when battling an eruption of dangerous half-breed creatures that might destroy an entire kingdom.
The Lesser Evil by E. A. Rappaport **978–0–9789393–5–9** **306 Pages $12.95**	Villagers and animals are disappearing from the coastal towns of the Cold Sea. The only ones who can restore peace are a necromancer, obsessed with bones and death, and a cunning thief who only cares about protecting his gold.
Lyche by E. A. Rappaport **978–0–9789393–6–6** **316 Pages $12.95**	An evil spirit, trapped within a volcano for ages, escapes its fiery prison with a vow to destroy all life. When no one else believes such devastation is possible, a young wizard and his companions must oppose the powerful creature on their own.
Voices from Below by E. A. Rappaport **978–0–9789393–7–3** **326 Pages $12.95**	When Halia and Xarun hear cries for help coming from their recently deceased friend, they must find a way to open a portal to the netherworld and send aid.
Whence Chaos Born by E. A. Rappaport **978-0-9789393-8-0** **308 Pages $12.95**	In a world ravaged by the awesome forces of nature, where homes and families are ripped apart by the winds and water of massive tsunamis and terrible earthquakes, a hero rises over the gale.
The Black Flood by E. A. Rappaport **978-0-9789393-9-7** **296 Pages $12.95**	Demons have breached the void and intend to claim the world as their own. Even with the combined forces of the Arboreals, Ferfolk, and Teruns, little can stand in their way.

www.ingramcontent.com/pod-product-compliance
Ingram Content Group UK Ltd.
Pitfield, Milton Keynes, MK11 3LW, UK
UKHW020132250726
13967UKWH00002B/611

9 781941 042137